Whom Gods Destroy

The Private Investigations of Josh Slim

Andy Lind

WHOM GODS DESTROY

The Private Investigations of Josh Slim

By Andy Lind

A SPECIAL THANK YOU TO YOU!

On behalf of everyone at Freedom of Speech Publishing, thank you for choosing Whom Gods Destroy for your reading enjoyment.

As a bonus and special thank you, for purchasing Whom Gods Destroy, you can enjoy discounts and special promotions on other Freedom of Speech Publishing products. Visit freedomofspeechpublishing.com/vip to learn more.

We are committed to providing you with the highest level of customer satisfaction possible. If for any reason you have questions or comments, we are delighted to hear from you. Email us at cs@freedomofspeechpublishing.com or visit our website at:
http://freedomofspeechpublishing.com/contact-us-2/.

If you enjoyed Whom Gods Destroy, visit www.freedomofspeechpublishing.com for a list of similar books or upcoming books.

Again, thank you for your patronage. We look forward to providing you more entertainment in the future.

Dedication

For Mickey and Max

Chapter 1

One lonely night in May, a body was found floating in the Rock River. To be honest, I wasn't surprised when I heard the breaking news come over the thirteen-inch flat screen that hid, hanging in the corner of the bar like a spider's web. After all, this wasn't just any city. This was Rockford, Illinois.

Rockford, Illinois, a city of close to two-hundred thousand people, two hours west of Chicago, and number two in the nation for murders in cities of its size. Rockford was no stranger to violence, as it ranked number five on the FBI's Worst Cities for Violent Crimes List. Still, it's home, and my home had crime and lots of it.

I used to care about my home. I used to care about all the crime it had. That's why I became a cop. It's why my initial instinct was to get off my seat and meet up with the boys, but I didn't. Instead, I continued to sit there, letting my dark-tan trench coat cover up a tear in the cushion of the barstool and holding the half empty glass of my dark, nearly black beer in my hand. I stared out the glass front door looking at the painted white letters that said, "Carl's" on it followed by four numbers that had faded away over time, with the words "East State Street" that would soon follow suit. I was retired, and I was slowly fading away much like the white painted name and address on the front door of the bar.

However, new events were about to come and change my life's own fading timeline. About a minute after the breaking news broadcast, there was a vibration in the right pocket of my trench coat. I pulled out the two-pound black dancing brick that was my cell phone and looked at it. The call I was receiving was from none other than Sergeant Joey Daniels of the Rockford Police Department.

"Slim, are you busy?" He always called me Slim, just like in the old days.

"Not really, Joey," I told him as I looked back at the half-empty glass of darkness in front of me. "I'm just sitting at Carl's having a beer." I took a quick glance around the bar to make sure that no one was close enough to hear my conversation. Joey Daniels wasn't the type of guy who would call you out of the blue just to chit-chat. "Why? What's going on?"

He was breathing heavier than usual. I didn't know at the time if that was because of the strange weather we had been having or because he was a little nervous. "I'm on Route Two, right on the river. A couple of teenagers were having some fun when they found a girl's body floating in the river, and well, I could use your expertise with this one. I would appreciate it if you got down here, fast."

"It's not my problem," I said before returning my eyes to my glass and telling him, "I'm retired, remember?" I hung up the phone before he could reply and took a sip of my beer. I wasn't in the mood to care about some dead girl. I wasn't in the mood to care about anything.

He called me back, but I quickly ignored the call and sent him to voicemail. Yeah, I'm one of those guys who actually uses it. After I had finished the next gulp of beer out of my glass, he sent me a text saying, "Call me or pick up!"

I rolled my eyes, played with my beer glass, and waited. I didn't want him to interrupt me in the middle of swallowing.

He called me again. My heart told me to pick up, and I listened, even though my lazy ass told me not to. "Joey," I said, "I don't understand what the big deal is? You've handled dead bodies before. We've handled them together. This shit should be nothing new to you."

"I know, but...," he said, nearly cutting me off. I could tell Joey wanted to tell me something, but he had either lost his train of thought or he was around people he couldn't talk in front of. He continued to hesitate for a moment as if he didn't want anyone else to hear what he was about to say.

I tapped my fingers impatiently on the bar a few times before my mouth decided to open. "But what, Joey?" I asked with an impatient tone in my voice. Old age does that to your tolerance.

"Give me a second."

"I've given you more than a few," I said, ready to hang up the phone again. "Remove yourself from whatever the situation is and talk to me in a spot where no one can hear you."

He was being distracted. I could only assume his attention was being pulled away by another officer. I could barely hear the two of them mumbling to each other, so I took advantage of the moment and took a swig of my beer while I waited for him to come back to our conversation.

"Slim, are you still there?"

I threw the last of the dark beer down my throat before I placed the empty glass gently back down on the bar so that I wouldn't draw any attention to myself. "Yeah, I'm still here!" I growled at him before I tucked my head into my chest and pulled my porkpie hat over my eyebrows in the hope that I wouldn't gain the notice of the other patrons.

The female bartender, who was half my age, came over and saw the empty glass. "Another one, Sugar?" she asked me before she placed her painted nails on the empty cylinder.

Normally, I wouldn't have refused the beer, or her, but I was on the phone with Joey and I still had no clue what was going on. So instead of accepting, I simply waved my hand at her, indicating I was done for the night.

"Are you busy?" Joey asked me once again, like he had earlier in our first conversation.

"NO!" I coughed into the phone before the same bartender brought over my bill, along with a pen that had appeared to have only a drop of ink left in it.

"Good, then you can meet me down by the river."

"The Rock River?" I asked before attempting to make a scribble on the paper.

"Yeah, that one. I'm down here with six other guys but this is a case where we could really use a guy like you."

I was becoming frustrated, with him and the pen. "You've got six other guys already down there with you and now you want me?"

"Yes, I want you here Slim."

"Hold on a second," I whispered as I grabbed my credit card and jammed it into my pocket. Then, I gently slid the bill with my barely scribbled signature to the edge of the bar before rolling the dead pen onto the floor behind the bar. In doing so, I figured I would give the other patrons something to look at instead of me leaving. As the men in the bar watched the thirty-year-old double-G breasted bartender bend over for the pen, revealing her G-string to them all, I snuck out the door. Once I was outside in the muggy May air, I could yell at Daniels as loud as I wanted to without anyone caring.

"I'm retired!" I shouted into the phone before giving him an earful. "Geeze, Joey, I don't understand why you and your men can't handle a simple job like this one!"

"You're right, you don't understand!" he shouted back at me. He took a deep breath or maybe two, I can't remember. What I do remember is that he was doing his best to calm himself down before telling me the following, "The dead girl we found in the river is none other than Melanie Cook, the daughter of the new Chief-of-Police, Peter Cook. You know him, he's the guy who took over shortly after you quit."

Chapter 2

The Rock River was the perfect place to dump a body. The three-hundred miles of icy cold liquid started in Wisconsin and stretched all the way to The Mighty Mississippi River. The watery racetrack ran parallel with Route Two, and because of that, I knew the boys weren't hard to find or get to. From Carl's, it would have taken the average person thirty minutes to get where Sergeant Joey Daniels and his men were. I made it in fifteen.

After arriving at the location of the scene, I called my old pal rather than text him. I hate texting. With a phone call, you either get someone right away or you don't. With texting, you have to sit there and wait for someone to type out a whole sentence when they could have just called you and spit it out in five seconds. Speaking of things that only take five seconds, that was how long it took Joey to pick up his phone. When he did, he didn't even get half of his hello out before I said, "Joey, I'm here. I'm going to need you to walk me past these reporters and the tape. I don't want anybody messing with me."

He did as I asked. He escorted me and once we were past the cameras and the mingling cops, I got as good a look at the body as I could with the crime scene spotlights. They were scattered through-out the area, highlighting what they could on this dark night. Even in her current state, and spotty lighting, I could tell she was a young woman. Heck, she didn't even appear old enough to drink. Her long blonde hair was a pile of wet spaghetti and the mud was the sauce. The left-side of her mouth had been cut with a knife, as was her neck, multiple slashes were going across it in the same direction. Her face was black-and-blue. The same color as the other bruises that were on her completely naked body. Whoever had done this, had turned this young, beautiful, blonde bombshell into a sick, mutilated, and twisted thing.

"We found her body just like this," Joey chimed in, "she was completely hogtied as you see her now. Her hands and feet all roped together like she's ready for a pig roast."

"And she's the pig," I said as I looked her up and down. "I'm glad to see none of you guys cut the rope?"

"We didn't." he said, before taking his hat off to wipe the sweat off his head. "We have just been waiting for someone with more authority to tell us what to do next."

"Where did you find her?" I asked before he had the opportunity to pull his attention away from me. There were a thousand distractions around us, and I didn't need Joey losing his focus.

He may have lost it for half a second, but he pulled himself back and answered my question. "The rope between her hands and her feet had gotten caught on the limb of that old hollow tree stuck out there in the river."

I looked at the tree, then looked at the body. It was too hard and too early to tell if someone had placed her body specifically on that tree to be found or if it happened to land and get caught there by chance. One thing was for sure though, she was cold, wet, and dead.

Joey bent down and asked me, "What do you think, Slim?"

I didn't know what to think yet and I didn't know what to say. All I could come up with were just two simple words, "Poor kid."

Joey wanted more than that out of me. "What was that, Slim? I didn't hear you." He'd heard me alright, but he wasn't in the mood to beat around the bush anymore.

I looked the girl up and down once more from head to toe. "To tell you the truth, I can't tell if this was done by a professional or an amateur."

"What do you mean?"

"Well, the bruises around the eyes and nose appear to have been caused by punches, but they weren't extremely hard blows to the face. It's as if whoever was hitting her was doing it just to rough her up a bit. The wounds by her jawbone appear to have been caused by some other object and it looks like that same object was used to cause the other bruises on the rest of her body."

"What about the cuts on her throat and by her mouth?"

Those threw me for a loop. "Well, they are all on the left side of her face. Whoever slashed her up did it quickly and carelessly. As if they were just waving a knife around hoping to hit something." I was done with the body for the moment. Now I wanted to move onto who had found her. I tilted my hat up and asked, "Who called in the body?"

Joey looked over his shoulder and nodded. "Those two kids over there."

I got a good look at them: A boy and a girl. The two of them looked about the same age as the girl they found in the river. They were standing by the ambulance, away from the cameras, and wrapped in blankets. "I'm gonna go talk to them."

I approached them slowly, allowing one foot to completely sink into the cold damp grass before I put the other one down. I kept my hands by my side, so they could see them. I also kept my posture as perfectly straight as I could, which is something I don't usually do. I tried to appear as non-threatening as possible. Obviously, it was hard for me to do.

"Are you kids, okay?" I asked, knowing they weren't. They had just seen a dead body floating in a river.

"Fine," the girl replied, which is the typical answer of a person who is anything but.

"Are you the girl's father?" the boy asked. It was obvious he couldn't see how old I was in the dark.

"No," I shook my head.

"Are you a cop?" the girl asked me.

To this day, I still don't know how to answer that question. "Not anymore," I told them before adding, "but I used to be."

"Well, who are you now?" she asked.

I gave them a summary of my story. "My name is Josh Slim. I'm a private investigator, who works with the police from time-to-time. I was a homicide detective until I retired six months ago."

"Why would the police bring out a private investigator?" the girl asked me. "Wouldn't they rather bring out a psychic?" Kids watch too many TV shows.

"I was a police officer for a little more than thirty years before I retired," I explained to them. "I know every one of the boys out here tonight and they know me. That's why I was called out here to help them investigate."

They nodded as though they believed me. That was a good sign. They were beginning to trust me.

"Now, I have a few questions for you both…"

"Shouldn't we have a lawyer with us before we say anything?" the boy asked me.

Smart kids. Too bad I was smarter. "I tell you what, I will ask you just three questions. I'll give them to you one at a time. If you would feel more comfortable answering the question with a lawyer present, just say, 'lawyer', and I'll respect your wishes."

The kids whispered to one another before agreeing to my terms.

"Good," I said before I began questioning them. "Question number one: Where did you two find the body?"

The girl pointed, "Over there. It was stuck on that tree floating in the river."

I looked back at the tree. I was able to get somewhat of a better look at the hollow tree now that I wasn't right on top of it. "That's a big one," I said out loud so the kids could hear me. I gave a detailed description of what I saw to make sure we were talking about the same tree. "It looks as though it had been struck by lightning sometime before winter and landed in the river. It's got that long branch sticking out of the water too."

"That's where we found the body," the boy said just before the girl gave him a sharp elbow to the ribs.

"Alright." I paused to give the boy a moment to recover from the jab. "Question two: Did you touch or move the body at all?"

"No!" They both said in unison firmly, seeming shocked I would even ask them that.

"Alright, good answer," I said before asking my next question. "Question three: Does anyone besides the police officers here and me know about the body?"

"No!" They responded in unison once again.

"So, nobody knows? You didn't take any pics and post them on any sort of social media?"

"That was more than three questions," the girl pointed out to me.

"Okay, you caught me," I admitted, "but you could say it goes along with the third question."

She hesitated for a moment before answering, "No. We didn't tell anyone or do any of that."

"Good," I said, tipping my hat.

"So, what happens to us now?" the boy asked me.

"The sergeant will take you down to the station and ask you a few more questions."

"What if we don't want to go?" the boy asked, fidgeting slightly. I could tell he was nervous.

I gave him something to be more nervous about. "You see those people behind the yellow tape?"

They poked their heads around the ambulance to see who I was talking about.

When their gazes came back my way, I started talking again. "Those people are reporters, and they would be more than happy to ask you more questions than either one of you could possibly imagine. The problem is, unlike the police, who will keep what you say confidential, the reporters, on the other hand, will take every word the both of you say and put it on every newspaper, website, and TV station they have."

"Wait a second," the girl said, "we would be on TV? We would be heroes. People would be talking about us all over the internet. We could end up trending!"

I didn't know what that meant, but somehow, I thought I had just shot myself in the foot.

Lucky for me, the boy chimed in, "I don't think that would be such a good idea." He was actually thinking with the head on his shoulders. I was impressed. "I mean, we're already in enough trouble as it is. If we talk to them, we may be in even more trouble than we already are."

"Smart thinking," I said to the boy before looking at the two of them and telling them, "Let's go."

Chapter 3

We were all at the police station by the end of the hour. The three-story brown brick building was a second home to Joey and me, but to these two kids, it was intimidating. It was the place they never thought they would end up seeing the inside of and it was a place they never wanted to be.

Joey, the shaky cop who seemed to have the need to be told what to do at every second was as solid as a rock now that he was at the station. He sipped some black coffee out of a paper cup he was holding before asking me, "What did you talk to the kids about, Slim?" His eyes didn't once move away from the glass that was looking in on the rooms the kids were in.

I let out a sigh before telling him the bare minimum, "I just wanted to make sure the kids didn't take a selfie with a dead body. That's all. I figured you or somebody else had asked them all the other important questions."

"Did they give you their names?"

"No, and I didn't ask either."

He took another sip of his coffee before telling me, "The girl's name is Mia Quarry. The boy's name is Troy Dublin. The two of them are eighteen. Other than that, they won't tell us much more about themselves."

"Of course, they won't." I explained the obvious to Joey, "Two kids find a dead body floating in the river. They decide to do the right thing and call it in. Then, before they can leave, you and your men swarm down on them like flies on shit, and you scared them out of their skin. They were already freaked out when they saw the girl's corpse. You guys just added more fuel to the fire."

"When did you become an expert on teenagers, Slim?"

I'm guessing he asked because he knew I didn't have any kids.

I rolled my eyes before giving him the only reason I could possibly think of. "My brother has got me teaching Sunday school, or high school confirmation, to be exact. He says the kids will keep me out of the bars, and my frightening presence will keep them off the streets."

"Good old Father Slim," he cracked a smile for a second before getting serious again. "So, how do you want to handle this?"

The window was large enough to give us both a glance into the two separate rooms where we had put them. I looked them both over before deciding. Troy looked like he was about to throw up. Mia looked like she just wanted to get whatever was coming over with and get out of there. I let out a sigh before I spoke, "Well, I think the kids themselves have already established who is good cop and who is bad cop, so I think I will talk to the girl first."

Joey was surprised by my decision. "Why her?"

Once again, it was apparent I would have to state the obvious for Joey. It was clear to me he was thinking like a parent and not like an eighteen-year-old boy.

I processed the thoughts going through my head. High school graduation was going to be next week. Troy more than likely didn't want to leave high school a virgin, so he takes Mia down to the river for a nice romantic evening. The rain from the previous night screws up his plans up a bit, but he still decides to go ahead with them anyway. They arrive at the spot, but then Mia sees something that startles her. She is curious and wants to see what it is, and boom, it's the body of a girl her age floating in the river with her hands and feet all tied up.

Instead of giving Joey every thought floating through my head, I just moved my neck and said, "The boy knows he's in enough trouble with his parents, as well as the girl's parents. All of the adults in his life are going to rip him a new one once he gets out of here, so he's nervous as heck. Our chances of getting a detailed story are better with the girl." I left the room so my words of wisdom had the opportunity to roll around in his brain for a bit.

Walking out of the room Joey and I were in and into the interrogation room where we were holding Mia was quite a change. Not just in temperature or in the atmosphere, as the interrogation room with its grey walls, open space, and cold air made it feel different, but in how being in the room felt. I went from talking to a grown man who was ready for anything, to a teenage girl who wasn't sure what was going to happen next.

"How's Troy?" Mia asked me before I even had the chance to sit down in the wooden chair on the opposite side of the table where she sat.

I was amazed. The girl sees a dead body, ends up in a quiet room in a police station with nothing in it but a table, two chairs, and a two-way mirror, and yet she is more concerned about her boyfriend than she is herself.

"He's fine," I answered. "He's sitting by himself in a room much like this one."

She smiled before she pulled a package of gummi bears out of her pocket. I didn't know why she had pulled the candy out of her pocket now, when she could have done so sooner. It may have been she was using the candy to cope with the situation she was in. I could relate; I sometimes get hungry when I am nervous.

I made an attempt to make her feel more comfortable by asking, "You mind if I have some of those? I haven't eaten anything all night."

She smiled, took a few more, and tossed the gold foil package to me across the table.

I got a couple down my throat before Mia's parents came through the door with Joey following right behind them. They quickly consoled their little girl.

I was leaning back and munching on the gummi bears when Mia's mother turned towards me and got in my face. "What did you say to my baby?"

I finished munching on my gummies before I answered the angry-looking woman's question. "I asked if I could have some of her gummi bears. They're delicious. You want one?"

"Who do you think you are?"

She demanded to know, so I told her, "Josh Slim, private investigator."

"Why are you talking to my daughter?" she asked while wrapping her brown hands around her baby's face. Then she smashed Mia's poor cheeks onto her chest and in her oversized boobs, which I was willing to bet was both uncomfortable and embarrassing for the teenager.

"She hired me to protect her," I said as I threw another bear down my throat.

"What are you talking about? She has no money."

"I accept gummi bears as a form of payment."

Mia managed to break free from her mother's grasp. She wanted to say something, but couldn't because her mother was doing all the talking.

"She doesn't need a private investigator. She needs a lawyer."

I knew laughing would be a bad idea at that moment, but I had the urge to do so. Over the years, I had dealt with so many paranoid people who think they need a lawyer for every little thing, when in fact, most of the time, they don't. Mia hadn't committed a crime, or at least nothing we could link to her yet. Still, I had to put things into perspective for Mia's mother. It's not like lawyers are up at all hours of the night just waiting for their cell phones to go off so that they can come down to the station to get someone who's just there to talk away from the police. So, I put my ankle on top of my knee before giving the misinformed Mexican lady a reality check. "Well, unless you know one who is up at this hour, she isn't going to get one right now."

"You can't hold her here. She is already scared enough as it is. Can't you see that she's just a frightened little girl?" she shouted, pointing to her little girl who did appear frightened, but not by me. Instead, she looked more scared by her parents and what they might say or, worse yet, do to her the moment she left our custody and returned to theirs.

To prevent the situation from escalating, I put the gummi bears down, stood up, put both hands on the table, and locked eyes with Mia's mother. "All I see is a brave young woman!" I shouted back at the lady who had been shouting at me. "Your daughter is quite possibly a hero. She has had more courage and common sense than ninety percent of the teens her age." I gave a quick glance over at Mia and got a good look at the wide smile spreading across her face before I turned back to face her sour-faced mother. "You're right, I can't hold her here, but we do need to have her fill out some paperwork before she leaves, or would you like to wait here for another eight hours so your attorney can hold your hand and fill it out with her? Cause lady, it's fifteen minutes after midnight, and I'm a single, old, retired man. I've got nothing to do till the Cubs game comes on at noon."

The Quarry's gave in and they sat by Mia as she filled out the paperwork. Troy Dublin's parents came into the station just as the Quarry's were leaving.

Talking with the Dublin's, it appeared that Troy's dad was more upset about the situation than his mother. His mother said she blamed Mia for the trouble she had apparently gotten her son into. Troy's dad knew his son better than that.

Once the Dublin's were gone, I told Joey I was going to head home.

"Slim," he stopped me by grabbing me by my bicep, "We need to take a look at the body."

Chapter 4

The ropes that held Melanie together had been cut and her naked body had been placed on a metal table in the morgue. The two-living people standing around the metal table were Coroner Katie Sickler and Detective Marcus Carlson. They were both happy to see me, but for different reasons.

Sickler, hadn't seen me in half a year. Her blue eyes lit up the moment she saw me and the blue frames of her glasses highlighted her eyes even more. She must've gotten the new specs while I was away. For her, me walking into that room brought back old times. Old times she probably thought she would never be a part of again.

Carlson, on the other hand, looked like a man who was about to lose his job and his lunch. He had seen many dead bodies in his life, but this one seemed to have given him a reverse tan on his dark brown skin.

Sickler broke the ice by greeting me with some small talk. "Hello, Slim, how are ya? How's the easy life? Must not be good if you're back here with us. How long have you been retired? Six months?"

"About that," I told her.

She opened her mouth to chat a bit more but stopped when she noticed all of us guys were paying more attention to the girl on the table than we were to her. "Well boys, get on some gloves cause this one is interesting." Interesting was the word Sickler always used when she couldn't figure something out. So, I knew whatever she was going to tell us was going to be a puzzle.

We each walked over to the wall where the boxes of gloves were hanging and grabbed a pair without saying a word.

As I was putting my hands into the tight rubber contraptions, I broke the uncomfortable silence by asking Carlson, "Does the chief know about this?"

"He's on his way." Which I took for him telling me yes.

If the chief did know, then I had an inkling this was going to be a coin toss for Carlson. As head detective, Carlson would either be assigned to the case or he would get the ass-chewing of his life. Maybe even both. I didn't know how Chief Cook ran the show around here, but I was sure I was going to get a crash course the moment he arrived.

Not knowing what to say next, I asked Carlson, "So, then, it is her?"

Carlson took a deep breath before he walked towards the table, avoiding eye contact with me. I don't know if he avoided my eyes so he could be matter of fact about the whole thing or if he was avoiding my face because he didn't want me to see any weakness in his. "We have every reason to believe so. I've seen the pictures on his desk enough times to be able to know his daughter when I see her."

"Well, let's hope everyone is wrong," I said while following him back to the table. Then I snapped the rubber glove against my wrinkly old wrist. Not just to wake everyone up, but also to show them I was ready to get down and dirty.

The three of us each took a different side of the table. This way, we could each see Sickler and the body without bumping into each other.

She waited patiently for all of us to get into our proper positions before she began her explanation of the examination. "Okay, boys, get ready to have some fun."

She started out in her usual fashion by leaning forward over the corpse and pointing to the places on the body she wanted us to specifically see. "For starters, there is no sign of rape or struggle. The ropes that were tied around her wrists and ankles were pretty tight, but as you boys can see, the marks are just one solid line."

Joey was a little confused. He gets that way sometimes. So, he asked Sickler a question, "So, what you're saying is she wanted to be tied up?"

"Possibly," Sickler said to make Joey feel good about his assumption, "but more than likely she was tied up right after died, as there doesn't appear to be any sign of a struggle."

"Why would anybody do that?" Joey asked. He was now more confused than he had been previously.

I gave the blunt explanation so nobody else had to. "Maybe she was into some kinky shit. Perhaps she wanted to be tied up. She could have been one of these girls who liked being dominated. Only problem was, she got screwed in a way she never expected to get screwed."

Sickler, being a woman, a mom, and an Evangelical Christian, didn't like where I was taking things, but she had to take what I was saying into account. Instead of expanding upon my assumption that this whole thing was just some strange sex fetish, all she said was, "The girl may have been tricked into being tied up, or her killer may have threatened her in some way, which made her think cooperating with him would be better…"

Joey cut her off to throw his two cents into the story. "Either way, it's a whole lot easier to throw someone into a river when they are tied up the way she was. Better for her to be wrapped up into a ball than to have her arms and legs flopping all over the place."

Sickler agreed with Joey and gave me a pointed look indicating the county cop could be right before she continued talking, "Now, take a look at the bruises on her face. She…"

Sickler's throat and finger were interrupted by a man coming through the double doors. The man looked ten years younger than me and ten-thousand times tenser. His shaved head was steaming, and I could almost swear his crooked nosed was crunched up so bad it would break itself again. His white skin turned to a freakish sunburn-like red as he walked, and his thousand-dollar skin-tight suit was tearing about at the seams the way a five-dollar one would.

The man marched over to the table, took one look at the body on the slab, and ten seconds later, two words rolled out of his mouth, "Get out." We didn't hear him the first time because it was almost as if he just growled the words, so he repeated himself, only this time, he screamed, "GET OUT!"

The four of us left the morgue in a hurry, and that was how I came to meet Chief Peter Cook for the first time.

We waited outside the room in silence. Joey and Sickler now looked as pale as Carlson did, only more so, because their skin was whiter to begin with.

I, myself, kept a cool head while I waited for the man to come out. I had seen these types of situations before, where a parent comes down to the station to identify the dead body of their child, and you never know how they are going to react. Some breakdown and cry, and others, like Cook, become so enraged they want to tear the room apart. Fortunately, he didn't, probably because the police chief in him knew how expensive it would be to repair the place.

About a minute later, Cook came back through the morgue's double doors to address the four of us. "My office, NOW!" he screamed, emphasizing the last word.

He led the way, and we followed him, but if you asked me, if anyone saw us, they would have thought the five of us were having a speed walking race down the hallway, with Cook having a good lead over the rest of us and with me being in last place, not caring at all.

Once we reached his office, he held the door open for all of us, and once my lazy ass was in, he shut the door before closing the blinds as well.

He gave us each a good look up-and-down before addressing the one person in the room who he knew could answer the question he was about to propose, "Alright, Carlson, who are these people, and what are they doing looking at the dead body of my baby girl?"

Sickler made the mistake of speaking opening her mouth. "Well, I'm…"

"I know who you are, Sickler!" Chief Cook snapped at her. He wasn't in the mood for jokes or for playing around. "I'm talking about these two." He took his finger and waved it around in the air as if it were a magic wand and he was about to cast some sort of spell on Joey and me.

Carlson somehow gained the courage to make the introductions in a professional manner that he always did his best to try and maintain with everyone. He started with Joey first, and I honestly wasn't surprised Chief Cook didn't know who Daniels was, as Joey avoided department politics like they were the plague.

All that mattered to Sergeant Joey Daniels was his job, and his men. "This is Sergeant Joseph Daniels of the Rockford Police Department. He and his men got the call about your daughter, I mean, they got the call about a body floating in the Rock River. He and his men were the first ones on the scene."

"And this guy?" the chief said, pointing his finger straight at me instead of waving it all round in the air like he did the last time.

Carlson didn't know how to introduce me, and he even knew it was a bad idea for me to be there, but we had known each other a long time, and he was almost sure Chief Cook had to have heard my name at some point. Carlson's face was still pale, but it was starting to return to its normal dark tone. Even though his skin tone was returning to normal, his speaking abilities had gotten worse. "This is…Detective Josh…Slim," he stuttered a bit before adding the word, "retired. He retired in November, about a month and a half before you became chief, sir."

Cook put his hands on his hips. He turned his lips to one side of his face. I could tell he didn't know what to make of me. I wasn't sure if he had even heard of me, but I could tell through his facial expression he was running my name through the data base in his brain. "A retired detective," he finally said. He repeated the phrase in a whisper only he could hear before he took his hands off his hips to ask me, "Tell me, Mister Slim, what have you been doing with your free time during these past six months?"

"Mostly drinking," I told him. I figured honesty would be the best policy in this situation.

My honesty did get a quick giggle out of Joey and Sickler, but Carlson was not amused.

Cook rolled his eyes. "Anything else?"

I knew how the department felt about people in my line of work, but I chose to stand tall and be proud of my new occupation. I took a deep breath and told the authority figure in front of me four words that summed up my new part-time occupation in a nutshell. "I'm a licensed private investigator."

"A private eye," he said in a sarcastic manner, which wasn't a surprise to me, "I should have known." He gave me another rundown with his eyes before telling me, "Well, you look the part."

I did look the part of a private eye. I was wearing a dark-tan trench coat with a matching porkpie hat. Underneath the coat was a dark-blue suit with light blue pinstripes. Below my suitcoat was a white dress shirt, the buttons hidden by a black tie that had two different sets of varying shades of blue stripes going sideways. I won't tell you what was underneath that, but I will tell you I was clean-shaven, and my breath smelled of Guinness and gummi bears.

I was about to shoot one of my quick lines back at him, but this was a guy who could have chosen to throw me out of the building or worse. So, I decided to be humble instead of humiliating. "Thank you, sir," I tipped my hat. "My dad always told me to dress for the job you want, not for the job you have."

A smile and a small cough came from the throats of Joey and Sickler.

Instead of addressing their reactions, Cook continued to address me, "Why are you here, Slim?"

I was about to say "To protect and serve" but instead, Joey put his foot and his mouth forward as if to come to my defense, "I called him, sir."

The chief was stunned. Why a county cop would choose to call a private investigator instead of a police detective or someone else higher up than him in the department, was beyond the chief's comprehension. Anyone could see Chief Cook didn't know the history Joey and I had together, which is why, when Cook asked Joey, "You did what?" I wasn't surprised.

Joey stuttered, but only for half a second. "I called him because I wanted his expertise with this." My pal the began listing off my credentials, so I didn't have to. "Chief Cook, I don't know if you know this, but Former Detective Slim had thirty-years with the Rockford Police Department. During his career, he solved more homicide investigations than anyone in this county. Everyone in this building knows him except you, and everyone in this room, as well as this building, can vouch for him. If that isn't good enough, he has even been asked to assist with cases as far west as the Iowa State line and as far north as Beloit, Wisconsin."

I grabbed Joey by the bicep. He had said enough. I didn't want him telling Chief Cook more about my past than I was comfortable with being exposed, and I especially didn't want him knowing about what happened in Beloit.

Where Joey seemed to leave off, Carlson suddenly chimed in. It was as if his balls had magically grown back within seconds. "Sir, with all due respect, I think we could really use former Detective Slim's help with this case."

"Have you lost your damn mind!" were the words that flew out of Chief Cook's mouth in reply.

I had no idea where Carlson was going with this, but I was more than willing to see where it went.

"I hate to say it, Chief, but with your daughter being the victim, that automatically makes you one of the suspects."

Cook's indoor sunburn was starting to come back. "Are you saying that I killed my only daughter, detective?" he asked through clenched teeth.

Carlson was walking on eggshells, and he knew it. He had to be careful about what he was going to say next. All of us in the room were watching him and waiting for his next slip up, but it didn't happen. Instead, he cooled the situation down with his unique way of putting things into perspective. "Not at all, sir, but if word gets out about this, then the press may portray it that way. If the press portrays you as a suspect, anyone you assign to this case could be considered a conflict of interest." He then turned to me and stuck his finger in my chest as if it was his way of getting his point across. "Having Slim on the case could be our best bet. He retired before you got here, so he has no connection to you. Plus, we can turn a blind eye to…" he paused for a moment, and I knew he was thinking about the ways I brought people to justice in the past so, he finished with the phrase, "…most of his methods."

Chief Cook thought about what Carlson had said for half a minute. It wasn't just me he was against, but the whole idea of a private eye handling this sensitive situation instead of one of his own men. It took him a moment, but he came around to Carlson's perspective of the situation. "Alright, Slim, you're hired."

There was a sense of slight cheer floating in the air between three of the people around me.

I felt the joy too, but all the sunshine and rainbows came to a halt when Cook asked me, "Do you have a gun?"

It took me a second to think because it had been half a year since I had kept one on me at all times. Then, I remembered, "I have an old .45 I bought at an antique gun shop in Volo a few months back. They told me it once belonged to somebody famous. It's nothing fancy, but it will get the job done if it comes down to it."

"Well," his eyes made their way towards the ceiling for a moment, "make sure it doesn't come down to it. You find that son-of-a-bitch and you bring him straight to me. I'll make sure he gets what coming to him."

I knew what he meant. He didn't have to go into details, and to prevent him from doing so, I just said, "Yes, sir."

"Do you need anything else from me?" he asked in a calmer, polite tone I had not heard come out of him until now.

"I have two requests." They were two requests he wouldn't want to hear. "I need to come over to your house and search your daughter's room. There may be clues in there as to who her killer might be."

He stood there silent for a moment. He didn't want to let me into his house, but he knew he had to. "Alright," he agreed. "Come over around five. That'll give you some time to search Melanie's room before my wife comes home. She doesn't usually get home until six and we usually don't eat dinner till around seven. I'll let her know a guest is coming over. What's the second request?"

"A nap."

Chapter 5

I got back to my apartment at about four o'clock in the morning. Instead of heading straight for my bed, I crashed on the recliner in my living room. I was so exhausted the only things I took off were my hat, coat, and shoes. I was no longer a man in my twenties or thirties where pulling all-nighters for the department was something I was used to. I was sixty-five now and didn't have the energy I once did. Now it seemed all I had the energy for these days was eat, drink, sleep, and dream.

Speaking of dreaming, I started having one almost the moment my head hit the back of my recliner. Most of the dreams I have I don't remember, but this one, I happened to remember every detail of it afterward.

In it, I was standing in front of the Rock River where I first saw Melanie's body. I was looking down into the cold black water when I saw her underneath all that darkness. She was moving towards me slowly, rising closer and closer to the surface of the water. Just before her body rose up to meet the air, her eyes opened. They became wide as she stared at me and so did mine as I stared right back. I was scared, but I wasn't terrified yet. The terror came when her hands left the water and her dead limbs reached up in an attempt to grab me. I'm still surprised I didn't wake up from the dream right then and there. I have been able to snap myself out of such nightmares, but I wasn't able to pull myself out of this one. I don't know if the inability to had something to do with the case or the fact that I was about to fight for my life.

As soon as her hands were on me, I fell backward and landed in the mud that lined the edges of the river. I grabbed two of the rocks behind me and used them to pull myself up just a little before somehow managing to make my way back to the grass by doing an old-fashioned crabwalk.

Her head and the upper half of her body rose out of the water, and I could have sworn she was coming to get me. But rather than come out of the water to attack me, she stayed in the dark liquid, the water barely touching her navel, giving her the appearance of a dead mermaid. Then, she stretched her arms out to me and cried, "Save me, Josh." She repeated herself, "Save me." Before she slowly returned to the abyss from which she had come, her wide eyes staring into mine the entire time.

I thought it was over, but it wasn't. I could barely breathe. I stood up, and from a pocket of my trench coat I took out the solid white handkerchief that my grandfather had given me before he passed away. I used my most precious material possession to wipe my face, and once I had finished, I heard a different female voice say to me, "Save her, Josh, I know you can." I turned to see who was speaking to me. The voice came from a headless woman, who I had not noticed was standing right beside me. She was wearing a thin backless purple shirt and a pair of black dress slacks that had holes in random places. She was holding her own head by its cold, dead, dark hair, which she had wrapped around her lifeless left hand. The head was slightly swaying back and forth in the air. The lips on the mouth of the rotting object moved by themselves. They continued to move as she spoke to me again, repeating the words she had said before, "Save her, Josh. I know you can."

I woke up suddenly in a cold sweat and grabbed my chest to make sure I was still breathing. After a few breaths, I pulled my cellphone out of my suit pants pocket and checked to see what time it said. It was a little after half-past eight in the morning. The sun was out, but the blinds on my windows were closed shut. I had spent most of my life in the darkness, becoming accustomed to it, but after the dream I'd just had, the light was starting to appeal to me. For a moment, I sat there and watched the sunlight peek in around the edges of my blinds.

I was starting to put my cellphone back into my pocket when I noticed something on my screen. I had a new voicemail. It was from Carlson.

"Yo, Slim, it's Carlson," the message began in the usual greeting Carlson used when he didn't have to be professional. "I'm just calling to tell you the Quarry girl called the station looking for you. She gave me her address. Give me a call back when you get the chance."

I got out of the chair, took a wiz, and gave him a call back.

He answered the phone by greeting me with what was apparently his favorite word, "Yo."

"Carlson," I shot back at him, "it's Slim."

His tone was cheerful and friendly. "Yo, buddy, how are you? Did you get some sleep?"

"About four hours," I mentioned while I massaged my eyes. I wasn't about to call it sleep as it seemed more like I'd had a four-hour nightmare.

He laughed. "You sound pretty good for a man with little-to-no rest."

"You sound pretty good yourself," I said before adding, "for a man who about five hours ago almost shit his pants in front of his boss." I didn't want him to get a word in, so I kept talking. "What did the Quarry girl want?"

A chuckle came over the phone. "Man, you like to get your punches in and go, don't-cha?"

I was going to throw another one at him, but I figured I'd let it slide, seeing as how he had some information I wanted.

"Well, she called the station wanting to know if she could talk to you some more about Melanie. She gave us an address."

I didn't feel like dealing with Mia's mother again, but I knew if I was going to solve this case, I had to. But I wanted to know first if there was an alternative to going there. "Doesn't she want me to just call her back?"

His chuckle now turned into more of a giggle. "No man, she wants you to come over to her house. I'm serious. Now, get ready to take down the address."

I fumbled through the kitchen drawers, frantically looking for a pen. After finding one, I grabbed the only piece of paper I had close to me. It was a receipt from Carl's a few nights prior, when I had given the hot bartender with the double-G boobs a big tip. She had written on my receipt the words *"Thanks for the big tip tonight, Sugar"* with a little heart, and I had put it on my fridge like parents do their kids' artwork.

I flipped it over to write on the back. "Go ahead, Carlson."

"All right, the address is nineteen ninety-eight Perdition Avenue. Do you know how to get there?"

I took a second to think. "Perdition? No. I have never heard of it. It must be part of a new subdivision."

"It is," he informed me. I could tell he wanted to laugh at me, but he didn't. Instead, he just said, "They built it on the outskirts of town. The easiest way to get there is to take Route Twenty to Meridian, hang a left on Meridian, then hang a left on Cunningham, and take that road to Perdition. You can only go right when you get to that road."

I wrote down the address and the directions as fast as I could before telling him, "Thanks. I am on my way there now." I grabbed my hat and coat before slipping on my shoes. Before walking out the door, I grabbed my gun from a nearby drawer as an afterthought, sliding it into a pocket of my trench coat as I left.

The house was about twenty-minutes from my apartment. I got there in twenty-five. Old people drive slow sometimes. When I arrived at the house, it appeared I wasn't the only guest there. There was a fancy Mercedes parked behind the other cars in the driveway. I didn't know whose it was, but I knew I was about to find out. I parked parallel to the curb out front, taking mental notice of the neighborhood I was in and the other vehicles parked and scattered down the street before getting out. I walked up the driveway to the two shades of gray cape-cod style house and rang the gold doorbell that was next to the fancy white door. Mia answered it before her parents did.

She hugged me with both arms. I didn't know how to respond but knew it probably wasn't a smart move to hug her back. She then grabbed me by the hand and told me to come inside the house. She led me past her parents and straight to the kitchen. The kitchen countertops were green granite, and the kitchen cabinets were pure white. Whoever designed this house clearly didn't make it for anyone who cooked. The cabinets didn't touch the ceiling but stopped a little more than a foot before it. It was here that Mia's parents had put their wine bottles to display their collection for all to see, but not touch or taste.

Although the kitchen was modern, the table wasn't. In fact, it looked designer vintage, like something from the seventies. It was long, with a white table-top and metal legs, and around the table were matching metal chairs each with a single white cushion. Sitting in one of the chairs was a man dressed in a suit that probably cost as much as the table and chairs combined. I also presumed he was the owner of the fancy Mercedes in the driveway.

Mia introduced the man simply by saying, "This is the attorney my family hired for me."

"Josh Slim," I said extending my hand towards him, "nice to meet you."

"Damien Marco," he said standing up and to shake my hand. "I'm the attorney for the Quarry family."

"That's nice, where's Polo?"

He rolled his eyes at me as if he had heard the joke a thousand times, and sat back down.

Mia's mother had been standing in the kitchen the whole time, watching us as if to see how the two of us were going to interact or rather how I was going to react. As soon as she saw things were going to be peaceful between us, she said, "Well, now that the introductions have been made, perhaps you two gentlemen would like some coffee." She moved away from where she had been watching, and Marco and I started to talk as I sat down in one of the chairs.

I didn't see the point of why I was called and asked here, but the lawyer felt it was his duty to tell me why he was here. "Mister Slim, I am here because the Quarry family asked me to come by to make sure that everything that happened down at the police station was handled appropriately and that you did not coerce or manipulate my client in anyway. Now, you told my client's parents that you are a private investigator. Is that true?"

My first thought was, *"Wow, and people say I talk too much,"* but I let the thought pass, choosing to do nothing but throw two words back at him, "That's right," as I tried to lean back in the uncomfortable metal chair.

"But you told my client you were working for the police department, did you not?"

"That's right."

"And that you were a former police detective?"

"That's right."

"And how long did you do that for?"

For the first time since this conversation started, I couldn't use my new catchphrase. "About thirty years."

"I see, so do I call you, Detective Slim, Mister Slim, or something else?"

"Just Slim," I said before giving him a nice long smile. "Slim will do just fine."

I could tell he didn't like the idea of calling me by my last name just by the way he made a small sour face. "I see," he said before he got to the point of all this. "Mister Slim, I am afraid my client cannot employ you, nor does she have any use for your services."

I shot a quick glance at Mrs. Quarry. She was smiling as she poured the water into the coffee pot. I knew this had been her doing, but I couldn't focus on her at the moment, so instead, I turned my attention back to the attorney. "Why not?" I asked Marco.

He smiled before giving me his prepared speech. "While you may mean well, you have done police work in the past, and you are even now working closely with the police, which means you could very well tell your police pals anything and everything my client tells you."

Clearly, I had to explain to him how my job works. "I'm a licensed private investigator and I am working with the police on this investigation. It's what I do. What I also do is protect my client's privacy so he, she, or it doesn't get accused of something they are not guilt]y of."

"And you don't see this as a conflict of interest?"

"No. I am a civilian now, but I also happen to be a civilian who knows everyone who works in that building downtown, so if you'd like some references…"

"I don't need references, Mister Slim," he said, cutting me off. "I respect your job and I need you to respect mine. My job is to keep my client out of your investigation as much as possible."

"As is mine," I pointed out to him. "Right now, Mia is simply one of the two parties who found a body in the Rock River, and I plan to keep her simply as one of those two parties unless she is hiding something from me that I should know."

Mrs. Quarry dropped one of the coffee cups on the kitchen floor. It shattered. She began to clean it up as fast as she could.

It was enough of a distraction to slightly break the tension between Marco and me. After a moment Marco took the opportunity to continue talking. "Mister Slim, let's be reasonable here. My client is eighteen years old. She has her whole life ahead of her."

"So did that girl in the river."

He scratched his head. "Mister Slim, I am here to find out what my client told you and to make sure you understand that from here on out, I will be advising my client on what questions she can or can't answer."

"And I am here to make sure you understand something," I said before opening up my trench coat and leaning forward. "I have a gun pointed directly at your kneecap, and if you don't quit with your overpriced attitude, I'm gonna pull this trigger and blow a hole right through it."

"Are you threatening me, Mister Slim?"

He stood up from the table like he was ready to fight me. Almost like he dared me to shoot him. If I did, the bullet would have gone through his one-hundred fifty-pound body the same way a sharp pencil could go through a piece of paper when pushed.

I accepted his challenge and stood up too. "Does this look like a threat?" I asked before I pulled out my gun and pointed it directly at his nose.

"I'm calling the police," Mrs. Quarry said before she went frantically searching for her cell phone.

"You are forgetting I am with the police!" I shouted to the woman but kept my eyes on the attorney. My voice went back to its normal, deep, scratchy tone. Now it was my turn to talk. It was my turn to give a lengthy speech. I was going to make sure it was longer than his was and that he was listening to every word of it. "Now, you listen here," I said as I stared at him. "I am going to say this slowly and clearly, so you understand. Your client is not wanted for anything. All she is doing is providing us with information to help us find the girl's killer. We are not even considering her a suspect. She and her boyfriend were just two people, at the wrong place, at the wrong time. If her overprotective, paranoid parents feel the need to pay you for protection, I hate to break it to them, but they just wasted their money. I realize you've got a job to do, and so do I. The only difference is, unlike you, I'm not going to let a declined credit card stop me from doing mine."

He could tell I wasn't going to budge. I could tell he was just going to keep pushing my buttons until I did something. He came up with a solution. "Why don't we ask Mia what she prefers?"

It was a good solution and I agreed to it.

Mia didn't need time to think. She knew exactly what she wanted, and she told us both, "Actually, I would prefer to talk to Mister Slim by myself."

Marco waited for me to put the gun back to the safety of my coat before he stormed out of the house, but didn't fully leave until he said something to Mrs. Quarry. I can only assume it was about the bill.

I looked back at Mia and shrugged. "Where would you like to talk?"

She made a nod towards the patio doors and we went outside to their backyard. I followed her to the edge of the yard where her childhood swing set was.

She sat down in one of the swings and invited me to sit down on the other one. "Come, sit," she said, patting the empty swing with her left hand.

I let out a deep sigh before telling her, "I haven't been on one of these since I was fifteen."

"Really? Why not?" she asked as if she wanted me to tell her a story.

All I told her was, "After I turned sixteen, cars seemed to be the only fun way to travel."

She smiled. "I love swinging. I love coming out here and just rocking back-and-forth. It helps me think."

"Is that why we're out here? So you can think?"

She looked down at her shoes before she spat out what she wanted to say. "That, and to get away from my mom. She's watching us through the small window in our kitchen. Don't worry, she can't hear us from this far away, and she can't read lips."

I knew her mom wasn't the type to have superhero style hearing. "I wasn't wondering about that. I was wondering about why you wanted me to come out to your house."

She looked at me with those big, kind eyes of hers. "Mom and I had a fight. She said she was going to call a lawyer and that I was to only talk to him. We screamed at each other for a while. Afterward, I ran into my room, slammed my door, and I called the police station hoping you'd be there."

That was the first time I saw a positive reason for a teenager having a cell phone. "Other than scaring off an attorney and pissing your mom off, was there another reason why you wanted me here?"

She paused for a moment before saying, "Yes. I have some more things to tell you about last night."

I tried to act surprised rather than sarcastic. "Oh?"

"Yes."

"Aren't you afraid of telling me more than you already have? It could get you into trouble."

"I know you won't allow me to get into any trouble, Mister Slim."

The kid hadn't even known me for a full day, and she was already putting all of her trust in me. I needed to understand how her little brain worked, so I asked, "Why's that?"

She looked at me with those kind eyes of hers again, and she told me a story, "You remind me of my grandpa. He was the toughest guy I ever knew. He was a Vietnam Vet. He didn't take any crap from anybody, but for some strange reason, I was the only girl who could melt his heart."

It was a little far-fetched, but not hard to believe. "You mean your mother wasn't even able to do that?"

"The man I'm talking about was my paternal grandfather, my dad's dad. My dad was an only child, and my grandpa was hard on him every second of every day. I always wonder if that's why he turned out to be such a pussy."

I couldn't help but laugh over what she said about her old man.

She started laughing too, but it was probably because I was laughing so hard. When we calmed down, she told me what she had been trying to tell me the whole time. "Seriously though, there is more to what happened last night than you think."

I was more than curious to know what she meant. I needed her to get to the point, but I knew she would in her own time. Instead of demanding a quick answer, like I had been known to do in my old age, I said one word and then let her talk. "Really?"

She came forward with a small confession. "Last night, Troy and I were planning to," she paused for a moment, "do it." She looked away. She was ashamed. I knew she was.

I was going to put my arm around her but I was afraid her overprotective mother was lurking nearby, so I didn't. Instead, I asked her, "Can I tell you something, kid?" She nodded, and I didn't continue until I had her full attention. Once I had it, I told her, "You don't have to keep it PG with me. I'm not your parents or your grandpa. To give you a little bit of comfort, I lost my virginity when I was about your age. It was in my car, in the girl's parent's driveway."

She was taken-a-back by it, maybe because she only saw me as an old man and not as once being a teenager like herself, but then she asked, "Did you regret it?"

"No," I went onto explain, "mostly because she has messed up her life more times than I can count."

Another small giggle came out of her before she continued on with her story. "Troy had it perfectly planned too," she said before she started to swing back and forth. "The spot he picked out had a fire pit. We were going to light a fire, cuddle by it, and as the fire went out, we'd do it in the dark. But when we pulled up to the spot, his brights shined right on the girl floating in the river. I got scared for a moment, but I thought it was a skinny-dipper, so I got out of Troy's truck to yell at her. Only she wasn't moving. It was then that I realized she was dead."

"Was it then that you called the police?"

"No," she shook her head. "Troy wanted to go somewhere else, but it's kind of hard to get back in the mood after seeing a dead body."

I nodded and agreed with her.

"I argued with him for a couple of minutes before we called the cops. If I was in Melanie's shoes, I would have wanted someone to call the cops for me too."

She threw me for a loop when she said the victim's name. "Wait a second, how did you know her name was Melanie?"

Tears began to form in her eyes. "Melanie Cook is, or should I say was one of the most popular girls in my school. When you're that pretty and that popular, anyone can spot you a mile away, even when you're dead and floating in the river."

Now, it was starting to make sense. The two of them didn't want to give any information to the police about knowing Melanie because then they would be considered suspects and possibly placed under arrest instead of questioned.

She continued to talk, "I also knew I could talk to you the moment you said your last name. You're Father Slim's brother. I could tell not only because of your last name, but also because you look like him, except he has a beard and glasses. Even though he has those features, you do look a lot older than him."

"That's because I am, by about four years of age and forty years of stress."

I rubbed my clean-shaven face with the hope some of the wrinkles in my skin would make their way to the surface.

I wanted to make her laugh now before things got serious. Because now, I was being put into a position where my client could be considered a suspect. I kept my cool and asked, "So, both you and Melanie went to the same school, huh?" I asked as more of a statement than a question. I paused for a second to think about my next question. I did not want to accuse the kid of anything, but I needed more information. My next question came to me within a few seconds. "Can you tell me anything I should know about Melanie?"

She shrugged her shoulders as though she didn't know what to say but knew she had to say something, and she did. "I can't tell you much. She was popular. All the boys chased after her. Not just because of her looks, but also because she always seemed to have money. She would even brag about it too."

I was confused by what she meant. "What do you mean by brag?"

I was asking a lot of questions. Maybe she gave me more information than I needed in the process, but if she did, it would be a good thing I had it. She let out a sigh before speaking. "I only had one class with her." It took her a second to remember which one. She eventually said, "Gym class," before she continued to talk about the interactions she'd had with the deceased. "I tried to be nice to her, but when someone constantly calls you things like Tom-Boy, Redneck, and Hick-Spic, and Lesbian

Mexican, you tend to avoid them. It's hard enough dealing with all the looks you get when your dad is white and your mother is Mexican, let alone the names that come with it."

I knew it was hard. Kids today are bullied a lot more than I ever was back in my day, and with all of this new technology, bullies become creative about how they hurt people and how they cover their tracks. In my day, kids settled things with their fists, and now, they settle them with their phones. Times were hard back then, but at least things were pretty black-and-white. Society has a lot of grey areas in it now, and I think that is what makes things harder. Growing up is hard. What is also hard, is explaining to your eighteen-year-old client that bullying is a motive for murder. I decided not to say a word, but instead, asked her, "Does anyone else besides Troy and you know about Melanie?"

"No," she said without hesitation. "I'm already unpopular enough as it is. Can you imagine the rumors that would be going around about me if people knew I was the one who found Melanie Cook's dead body floating in the river?"

I didn't want to imagine. The kid had been through enough already. "How do you keep your cool so well?"

"Only three opinions matter to me: God's, Troy's, and my own. Most of the time, they are not in that order."

"You really do love that boy, don't you?

"More than anything."

"Tell me, what is his opinion about Melanie Cook?"

"He doesn't really have one," she said before smiling, "he's too focused on me."

I thought about what she had just said; I wondered if it was possible that Troy had murdered Melanie and that he had taken Mia out to the river last night to show her what he had done. Only it backfired on him. If Troy did murder Melanie, was Mia just covering for him? If she had murdered Melanie, would Troy do the same and cover for her?

"So, where do you go from here, Detective?" she asked me, which snapped me out of one of my thoughtful funks.

I looked up at the sky in the hopes God would give me something inspiring to tell this teenager, but nothing came, so I shot from the hip and told her, "I think I'm going to go investigate the spot where the two of you were last night before it rains."

She agreed it was a good idea. "Will you let me know if you find anything?"

I didn't know if it would be a smart idea to tell her. She was already too involved in this as it was, but I told her anyway. "I already did. I hate to break it to you kid, but you are more of a suspect than you think."

She was confused and starting to get scared. "What do you mean? I don't understand!"

I knew I had to explain things to her in a sensitive way that she could understand. I also needed her to stay put while I gave my explanation. I thought about grabbing her arm so she wouldn't run away, but I figured my actions would only frighten her more, so I used my soft and sweet voice and I leaned towards her ear so she could hear what I was saying. "Listen, kid, when I first met you, all I knew about you was that you were a girl with a bad case of bad luck. Now that I know that you were Melanie's classmate and you were bullied by her, I may have to keep you in the dark with the investigation. The more details you know, the more it will make you look like a possible suspect."

Mia didn't like what she was hearing, but she knew it was the truth. She appreciated me telling her because she now knew what questions she would have to answer if the police showed up at her door. But before she'd answer them, she would have her mom call the lawyer back.

I looked up to notice her mother peeking out the window and watching us. I had already overloaded the kid, and knew if I said anything more, it might have pushed her over the edge. So, I stood up from the swing and told her, "I better get going. I'm on a tight schedule, and the possibility of rain has made my schedule even tighter."

She stood up too and hugged me once again, throwing both arms around my oversized torso. Once again, I didn't know what to do. So, I just took one of my hands and patted her on the back. I look toward the window and made eye contact with her mom so that she knew I knew she was watching us.

As soon as she saw me, she walked away from her post. I was positive Gladys Kravitz from "*Bewitched*" was running to tell Abner or someone else.

Rather than go back into the house, I decided it was best to walk around the outside and head back to my car that way. I wasn't more than ten feet away from my car when I heard someone yelling at me, "Since when do cops give children hugs?" Sure enough, it was Mrs. Quarry.

I turned around and told her, "You saw what happened." I didn't walk towards her because she knew I had my gun on me. I didn't want her to think I was going to attack her, so I stayed put and pointed out the fact that her kid had made the first move.

She walked towards me huffing-and-puffing but stopped in the middle of the driveway as though she suddenly remembered I was carrying a gun. She tried to keep calm, either because she didn't want me to pull out the old .45 or didn't want her neighbors to think she was nuts.

From the point where she stopped, she asked a simple question. "Mister Slim, Detective Slim, whatever you want to be called, do you really have my daughter's best interest at heart?"

I knew that, deep down inside, she was just another mother hen trying to protect her chick from being eaten by some sinister fox. I gave her the most non-threatening smile I could force my face to make. "Ma'am," I said to her. "I have all of my client's interests at heart, and I am doing my best to solve this case without dragging your daughter further into it."

"Do you have kids, Mister Slim?"

"No," I told her. "I don't. I never got the chance to." I said, in the hopes she would think I was purer than I really was. I don't know if she bought it or not, but it was worth a try.

"Well, I am going to tell you that Mia means the world to me." She went on to tell me how she'd had a rough pregnancy with Mia and how after she was born, her doctors had told her she would never be able to have another child the way Mother Nature intended. When she finished her story, she started to tear up, but held the tears back in the same way Mia had done when I talked with her. Mrs. Quarry concluded her speech by saying, "She is my world, Mister Slim. Don't destroy it."

I tipped my hat towards her and gave her some assurance. "Ma'am, my job is to solve this case and protect your world at the same time. I am trying my absolute hardest to do both."

"You better," she growled me before she let the tears loose. Then, she quickly turned around and walked back into her home so I wouldn't see her cry.

I did nothing more but turn around and shake my head. As I began walking to my car again, I noticed out of the corner of my eye that there was a black Cadillac SUV with one person in the driver's seat, not too far down the street. It had been sitting there the whole time I had been inside the Quarry house. Right before I got to my vehicle, the person in the driver's seat turned on the engine and drove away. I had a gut feeling that it wouldn't be the last time I would see that car.

Chapter 6

I drove out to the place on Route Two where I had been the previous night. The yellow police tape was still up, but no one was around except for the cars passing me by. So, I decided to look around a bit. The crime scene I had seen last night looked a whole lot different in the daytime. The ground was dry for now, but I knew it would rain again soon and I didn't want to be stuck outside when it did, so I made my investigation as fast as I could before both the wrong people and the rain found me.

I will admit, I was a bit hesitant about going there after the dream I'd had. I was waiting for a dead girl to pop out of the water and reach for me. I made the plan to keep my feet on the grassy area for as long as I could while I was there.

When I walked past the tape, the first thing I noticed was the fire pit where Mia told me Troy had planned for the two of them to have their romantic evening together. When I got close to it, I put my hand on the ground and felt around the hole. Nobody had used it in a while, and the area was still wet, which was a good thing because it proved that part of Mia's story was the truth. Now it was time to see if another part of her story checked out.

I made my way toward the tree where the two kids had seen Melanie's floating body. Walking around by the river's edge in dress shoes is never a good idea, but this was the only pair of footwear I owned, so I didn't have much of a choice. I reluctantly made my way past the sandy mud and rocks before putting my left foot onto the tree. When I lifted up my right foot up and tried to place it on the tree as well, I slipped, and my foot landed right in the river. I spat out a few curse words. Not only because of the fact that my foot was now soaking wet, but also because I was afraid zombie Melanie was going to come out of the water and grab it. I grabbed ahold of the tree with both hands and pulled myself up on it a little further and onto the tree. I was surprised the tree was able to support my weight and was even more surprised I was physically able to climb it. I carefully moved further up the dead, hollow piece of wood to get a closer look at the branch that was sticking out of the river, the one that caught Melanie's body.

A thought entered my mind, *"If either Melanie or Troy had chosen to place Melanie's body in here, it would've taken the two of them to do it. One of them would have had to be willing to get completely soaked, but both of their clothes were dry when the police arrived."* The thought of the two of them bringing extra clothes with them and throwing the wet ones into the river did cross my mind; however, the chances of the police finding them would have been high.

I tried to think of any other way they could have gotten Melanie's body into the river if they were the culprits, but I couldn't. Even if the two of them were in a small boat, it would have taken some skill for two people to lift a dead body out of a boat and place it just perfectly on the branch where it could get caught. If this was set up, it was a damn good one.

I turned my head to look up the river to check how it was flowing. The current would've been strong that night because of all the rain we'd had. That would make setting a body on the branch a dangerous job. I doubted anyone would have taken that chance. It would have been possible for someone to just dump the body further up the river, and then the current just pushed it all the way down here, where it eventually caught on the branch. But where would they have dumped it from?

I considered all of these before I got off the tree. I walked around the crime scene a few more times, checking the grass carefully, making sure nothing was on the ground. If any sort of foreign object was found, it could incriminate Troy and Mia even more. I carefully inspected every inch of the damp green blades I walked past. I had only one chance before the rain started, and it was coming soon, as the sound of thunder was now above my head. I came to the conclusion that either nothing was dropped, or the investigation team did a pretty good job of picking everything up.

There was only one logical scenario as to how the body got stuck on that tree. I was convinced the Melanie Cook's body had floated downstream and landed on the branch, hooking itself there to eventually be found.

Hopping in my car, I drove north on Route Two until I came to the far south end of Main Street. Before I made my turn, I looked over to the right and saw the same black Cadillac SUV I had seen on Perdition.

It was parked on the side of the road right before the small bridge that started at the light and went all the way to Airport Drive, which was the next street. The driver was standing outside of the vehicle, closer to the bridge. He was looking down the river with a pair of binoculars. I got a good look at him as I sat in my car. He looked a little bit taller than me. Just so you know, I'm six-foot-two, and this guy had to be about six-foot-four. He was also heavier than me. Just so you also know, I weigh two-fifty. This guy looked like he weighed well over three hundred pounds. He was caucasian, with dark curly hair, appeared clean-shaven, with big hands and an even bigger gut. If he'd had sideburns, he could have passed for Andre the Giant Junior. He looked over and saw my car. His eyes turned towards the sky as it started to rain. After putting the binoculars back into his pocket, he slowly walked back to his car.

I wanted to follow him, but I didn't. Something in my gut told me he would have noticed, and in the private eye business, the last thing you want to be is noticed. Instead of making a right turn in the direction he went, I went straight and pulled into the gas station that was directly in front of me. While I was there, I figured I would grab a snack. After all, I hadn't eaten anything since the gummi bears Mia gave me early this morning, and my stomach was starting to notice the absence.

The place was a living, breathing hypocrisy. Clean floors with dust on the shelves that only seem to be removed when customers took old products off, and employees put new ones on. Brand new magazines were stacked neatly on a wooden rack that looked like it was put together by a ten-year-old boy scout. Bullet resistant glass gave the counter more security than a bank, but the clutter on the counter was enough to make even a hoarder cringe.

After grabbing some stale coffee and overpriced beef sticks, I walked up to the register and casually asked the multi-color haired girl behind the secure glass if anybody did any fishing off of the bridge that was adjacent to their parking lot and the river.

Rainbow Brite shook her head. "They aren't supposed to. We've been told to call the cops if they do."

"Do you guys ever call the cops on them?"

"Not really," she shrugged. "It's mostly out-of-town people or hicks who fish off that bridge. I've been told the only reason they fish off the bridge is that the current is fast, and it's easy to catch the fish who are swimming downstream. We usually only call the cops on them if they're dicks to us. Other than that, we leave them alone, for the most part. Besides, we can't really see the license plates from here, and our cameras don't pick up anything past the pumps."

I walked over and looked through the glass double doors of the building. Indeed, there was enough shoulder room on the bridge for someone to park there, get out of their car, and toss Melanie Cook's body into the river. The question was, could someone sitting behind the glass and clutter-covered counter see such an act being done. I had to know, so I turned around and ask Rainbow Brite, "But you can see the cars on the bridge from here?"

The more questions I asked, the more distrusting of me she became. She knew I was up to something, but she couldn't put her finger on it just yet. "Yes…yes, you can."

"Even at night?"

"I guess so."

She stayed silent for a few seconds, but it didn't take long for her to ask the question people like to ask when I start asking too many of my own.

"Say, are you a cop or something?"

"Yes," I said in a blunt manner. There was no sense beating around the bush any longer.

Her demeanor changed. Her eyes hit the floor and spun in so many directions someone would have sworn she was possessed by Satan. I had seen this kind of behavior many times before. Even people who get pulled over for something as simple as a tail-light being out were known to check their P's and Q's before the officer gets to their window. It was probably a good thing she acted the way she did because I could smell the scent of weed coming from behind the counter the moment I walked into the store.

I decided to use her behavior to my advantage. I marched back over to the counter and gave her my spiel, "I am a cop. I'm out here investigating a murder. A body was found in the river last night, and I need to know if anybody saw a car pull over on that bridge last night. If there was a car, I need to know what kind it was."

My monologue made her nervous, and I knew it. She knew it too. But at least she stopped spinning her eyes around and gave me her full attention. "I...I don't know. I wasn't working."

"Well, then who was?"

"I can't tell you that."

"Why not?" I asked, using my mean voice. Thunder boomed outside, adding a nice effect to the situation.

"We...we aren't supposed to give out other people's schedules," she said, giving me the best excuse she could come up with.

I wasn't buying it, and I decided to be a hard-ass and give her an ultimatum. "I'm not asking you for a schedule. I'm asking you, 'Who worked last night?'. Now, either you will answer my question, or I will call a K-9 unit and have a dog sniff through your car to find all that weed you've been hiding."

"Okay, okay, I will tell you." She grabbed a clipboard that was hanging on the wall adjacent to the register. She ran her finger down what I assumed was a schedule, and when she found the information I was looking for, she gave it to me. "Zach worked last night. He works again tonight, too. His shift starts at eight and ends at two."

I gave her a sleek smile and returned my voice to its normal tone. "Thanks, kid, and if you tell him I'm looking for him, I'll come back on your shift and throw the book at ya for all that weed you've been smoking."

"The next governor is going to make it legal you know," she shot back.

"Well, he ain't been elected yet," I shot as I watched her ring up my stuff. After paying for it, I headed for the glass double doors. I turned around and used my butt to open it. I wanted to give the girl one last smile as a way of thanking her for the information she had given me. I also wanted to see if she was going to get on her cell phone and give Zach a heads up.

She didn't. She also didn't say a word to me, which was fine, even though I was expecting some sort of smart-ass comment to come out of her mouth as I made my exit. Instead, she pulled out a can of air fresher from underneath the counter and sprayed herself with it.

"Good girl," I thought to myself as I wiggled back to my car through the now pouring rain.

Chapter 7

I still had some time to kill before I was supposed to be at Chief Cook's house, so I decided to be a good Catholic boy and go to Confession and Mass. My brother's parish was on the northeast side of town. I had to get on the highway to make it there on time, which I wasn't too thrilled about cause people nowadays drive like maniacs, but I made it there just fine.

The outside of the church looked more like a giant stone circus tent rather than a massive structure designed to reach Heaven. The church was in the shape of a circle, and the bottom half of it was made out of brick. The circle of bricks stretched about ten feet high before a pyramid shaped roof covered all of it. The cross on the top of the roof, and the electronic sign by the road with the parish's name on it, were the only visible indicators letting people know that the hideous building was a church.

Inside the massive structure, the oversized painted marble statues seemed out of place when one looked at the ceiling covered in wood. The stained-glass windows with their multi-colored patterns instead of Saints seemed even more out of place. The only thing that seemed to fit in with the building was the tabernacle, located in the center of the altar. I really do wish the people who designed Catholic churches would make up their minds. Either choose to go back to how things were before Vatican II or become so modern that churches don't look like churches anymore. Instead of choosing to look like large classrooms where no one has their own individual seat. Until traditional Catholics and modernists can get along, we dear and practicing faithful, have to put up with this ugly mix of designs.

I stood in line for Confession, which towards the back of the church. The confessional looked like a big wooden box with three doors. The center door was the biggest of the three. The two other doors were smaller but equal in height. In the middle of the center door was a tan-colored cross, and I knew behind that door was my brother.

There was only one guy in front of me and two other guys in the booth, one on each side. That was another thing I noticed had changed over the years. It seemed more and more men were going to Confession. I guess it's because in this day and age men have more to apologize for than women.

Two minutes after the guy in front of me entered the confessional, the guy on the opposite side walked out. I walked through the door and entered into a tiny room with three white walls and a fourth wall that was completely wood, a small window cut out in the center of it. Even the confessional booth was completely mismatched.

I knelt down on the wooden kneeler covered in soft green padding and stared at the small window. Covering the window was a black screen, and in front of the black screen were tiny centimeter-thick bars that crossed one another to form X-shaped patterns. After staring at the small window with the X-crossed bars for a few seconds, I heard the sound of a small door sliding. When the door stopped, I saw a low light coming from behind the opaque screen behind the pattern of X-crossed bars. The priest said, "May the Lord be on your lips and in your heart. May He give you the grace to make a good Confession. How long has it been?"

"Hello, Jacob," I said to my brother instead of answering the question.

"Josh," he sounded surprised. I couldn't see it, but I was willing to bet the look on his face was more shocked than his voice. "What are you doing here? You know you can't come to me for Confession."

"I'm not here for Confession," I told my brother, hoping he would chill out.

He did after a few seconds but still fumbled over his words for a moment. He then leaned closer to the screen separating us and let out a harsh whisper, "Well, get out of here and let someone else in then." I could tell he was already getting frustrated with me.

"I can't do that."

"Why not?" he growled. My brother was beginning to use his version of an angry voice.

I was loving every minute of it, and decided to push his buttons a little further. "Because I need to talk to you."

"Well, talk to me some other time, Josh. I'm busy."

"You are not busy."

"I am too. I'm hearing Confessions."

"There's nobody else in line. I made sure of it. I'm the only one."

He hesitated for a moment. I knew what he was doing. He was checking to see if what I said was true. Coming back a few seconds later, he knew I was telling the truth. "You're right. Nobody is on the other side. You are the only one."

"See," I told my brother. "Take it from someone who spends his life outside of the box. All the people who want to go to Confession come when Confession begins. All the people who don't want to go to Confession show up right before mass is about to start."

He let out a heavy sigh, and his voice returned to its normal speaking tone. "Okay, Josh, you have my attention. What do you want?"

I knew my brother was a sensitive guy, so I did my best to soften the bad news. "Did you hear about the body they found in the Rock River last night?"

"Yes, I did. What about it?"

"Well, I know you are vice-principal of the high school, and I know you know a lot of students, but I was wondering if you knew of a girl by the name of Melanie Cook? You see, she was the dead girl found in the river last night and…"

"Oh no." Those two words said it all, I knew everyone involved went to the Catholic high school he was partly in charge of.

I didn't want to give him the details; I knew what a weak stomach my brother had so, I tried to cut to the chase, keeping it simple. "Yeah, big oh no. She's the chief's daughter and…"

Before I could get through my little speech, my little brother interrupted me. "You don't understand. I have a lot to do now."

The list of to-dos that came out of his mouth shocked me. Once again, my brother, a priest who was supposed to be selfless, was being selfish. He told me how he had to meet with the teachers and send a letter to the parents. That there needed to be a special Mass said for her, and how he had to accomplish all of these tasks the week before graduation.

"Will you shut up and stop thinking about yourself for a minute?" I shot back to him to get him to stop his stupid ranting. "Gosh, sometimes, I think you only became a priest just so you could have a cushy lifestyle, get a ton of free stuff, and stop being rejected by all the women you use to ask out on dates." I took a deep breath. Gosh, it felt good to get that out of system, but I knew if I continued to insult my brother, he would close the window on me. So rather than fight him on the subject of his narcissism, I got us back onto the situation at hand.

"Listen, nobody knows the body found in the river last night was Melanie Cook. The police department is keeping this as hush-hush as they possibly can. I have been hired by the police to solve this case as quickly and as quietly as possible. Chief Cook wants this wrapped up before the truth about her identity comes out." I left out the part about how Troy Dublin and Mia Quarry were involved and how I was trying to wrap this case up before the police considered Mia a suspect. It was bad enough my brother now knew that I knew one of his students. Telling him I knew three would have sent him over the edge.

"Well, I'm glad you've been able to find work, Josh," my brother said in an almost sarcastic manner, "but why would they hire you?"

I gave him a brief rundown, telling him how Detective Carlson was afraid when word got out that the body found in the river was the daughter of the new chief-of-police, the press would have a hay-day with the information. I told him no matter who it was that was taken into custody, people would question whether or not it was a conspiracy against the person who got arrested. Plus, if Cook hired one of his favorites to cover the case, it could look like a coverup.

"I take it people don't like the new police chief?"

I didn't know if that was true, but I did tell my brother about my brief encounter with Chief Cook.

"I see," was his response. "So, nobody knows that it was Melanie Cook who was found in the river?"

"Nobody but you, me, and a few people at the department," I took a deep breath because I didn't want anyone else knowing about the kids' involvement, but if I didn't tell him and he heard it from some other source, he would have been hurt, so I mumbled, "and two of your students."

"Which ones?"

I knew I could trust him with need-to-know information. After all, he had been hearing Confessions for years. "Troy Dublin and Mia Quarry."

"How do they know?"

I broke the bad news to him. "They found the body in the river."

"Dear Lord!" I could feel his shock through the fragile wooden walls of the confessional, and I knew my brother was crossing himself.

"Do you think they could have murdered Melanie?"

I took a deep breath before answering his question. "To tell you the honest truth, Jacob, I don't want to believe it, but seeing as how Melanie bullied Mia, both her and Troy are my top suspects."

"I don't think they did it," my brother said, being the naïve priest who believed his students could go from sinners to Saints with the flip of a switch said with a tone of confidence. "Troy and Mia keep to themselves most of the time outside of class. They really don't associate much with other students."

"I believe you on that, Jacob, but let me tell you something about bullies and being bullied."

I gave him some insight into bullies. How they will do little things just to annoy or inconvenience another human being who is different or weaker than they are, and how all of those things eventually add up. When they do add up, well, everyone has their breaking point. That's when the person being bullied finally takes action, and they don't always do so in a small way. They can take action in a big way, and if anyone ever had any doubt about that, all they had to do was tune into the latest school shooting.

He hummed a bit before admitting, "You do have a point there, Josh."

"If Mia was being bullied by Melanie, you can guarantee that she told Troy about it. Troy could have possibly taken the situation into his own hands. No man, no matter how good or bad he is, wants to see his woman treated poorly by someone other than him."

"Do you have any other suspects besides Troy and Mia?" I could tell my brother was asking me because he wanted to get off the subject of me portraying his students in a negative light.

"Chief Cook is a suspect, of course. I hate to think that a man would murder his own daughter, but I have to keep him in mind. Also, I've been seeing this guy in the same places I've been visiting. I don't know anything about him. All I know is he is a big man, and he drives a black Cadillac SUV."

"A black Cadillac SUV!?" my brother echoed. "Oh, Josh, of all the cars you had to mention, why did it have to be that one?" I had triggered something in his brain. He knew something about that car.

I had to get it out of him. "What do you mean?" I reminded Jacob that I hadn't been holding anything back from him, and I gave him a slight threat through the little covered window separating us.

My younger brother's voice cracked just like it used to when he was going through puberty. "It's nothing, Josh. It's just…I should've known that guy was more trouble than he appeared to be."

He was good at keeping secrets, but I couldn't let him keep this one. I shouted at him for a few seconds until he finally cracked.

He started to tell me a story he didn't really want to tell, but I needed to hear, and he needed to tell it to me. I could tell this was something he was hoping to keep to himself, but it was time to let it out.

He went on to inform me that for the past couple of weeks there had been a black Cadillac SUV parking in the student parking lot. It would get there and park anywhere between ten and fifteen minutes before school let out. My brother noticed some of the prettier, more popular girls, including Melanie, would run up to the SUV after school had ended. They talked to whoever was inside the vehicle. After the girls would finish talking to the mystery person, the SUV would drive away. At first, he thought it was one of the popular girl's parents, but when he noticed no one ever got inside the vehicle, he became suspicious.

I asked him what he did about it.

"I waited for the car to pull into our lot one day, and I went outside to talk to the person driving it. I didn't expect to see a man driving the car, let alone a man of his size."

I was impressed when I heard my brother didn't back down from the challenge, and for the first time in a while, I was proud of him.

As I smiled from behind the wall, he continued to tell me what happened. "I asked him if he was one of the student's parents. He said he was Melanie's uncle. I told him Melanie didn't have an uncle, which is true. He didn't like it that someone caught him in a lie, especially a priest."

For the first time since his sermon on how drinking in moderation was not a sin, he had my undivided attention. "What did you do then?" I asked to get him to continue to talk.

"I told him if I ever saw him in my parking lot again, I would call Melanie's dad and that Melanie's dad was the chief of police." He took a deep breath before spitting out his catch-phrase, which was, "Oh my gosh." I could tell a horrifying scenario had entered into my brother's brain, and the next words out of his mouth confirmed my assumption. "Do you think by me giving him information about Melanie's family, I could have led her straight to her death?"

I didn't want to lay a thought that bad on my younger brother's conscience even though it was tempting to put him on a guilt trip. So, I told him I was mostly certain that the status of Melanie's father wasn't the reason she was murdered. However, I kept the possibility of it in the back of my mind. But for now, I needed to hear the rest of what my brother had to say, so I persisted. "Tell me, what happened next?"

He told me he never saw the car or the man in the school's parking lot again, and I believed him. He assumed the big man was just some guy selling drugs to students in the parking lot. Even though he got rid of the guy, the thought of his students doing drugs was enough to keep him up at night. He called Melanie's dad and asked him if he could have one of his men bring some dogs into the school and sniff the lockers for drugs. Of course, he didn't have the heart to tell him Melanie could have been one of the students involved. When his men found nothing, my brother's heart slipped back into place, and he dropped the whole thing. He didn't tell a soul about Melanie or the man in the black SUV.

"So, are you one-hundred percent sure about Melanie being one of the girls who talked to the man in the black Cadillac?" I asked, and after he told me again that she was, I repeated the question to make sure.

He told me, "Yes," a second time and I knew for sure that, he was positive.

Jacob reminded me of the time. He only had a few minutes left to chat with me before he had to get ready for Mass. He asked me if I had any more questions for him and the only one to come to my mind was, "Can you tell me anything about Melanie that would help me solve this case faster?"

He let out a sigh, "I really don't know, Josh."

He went on to tell me how Melanie was a popular girl and popular girls only get into enough trouble to keep themselves popular. They don't do anything worth a phone call to their parents. He described Melanie as a girl who came into the high school as a senior. She didn't grow up with the class like all the other students did, but she did have one advantage over them all, she turned eighteen before the other students did. That was because she had the earliest birthday in the class. The only major trouble she got into was buying cigarettes for her peers. When my brother found out about it, he brought her into his office, but he had a few of the other teachers in there so she wouldn't accuse him of something, which was a smart move on my brother's part.

A few of the teachers, along with him, talked with her and explained to her what she was doing was wrong. They also gave her this lecture about how even though she was a legal adult, she still was not allowed to smoke on campus. She tried to justify herself just like any teen would and when she did, my brother showed her the school's policy along with a petition signed by all the faculty to make the school a one-hundred-percent smoke-free campus.

"I really don't care about your policies and procedures, Jacob," I growled at him through the small screen in the hopes of getting him off his tangent. "Did you notice any suspicious behavior from Melanie lately?"

"Other than the fact that she had been flaunting her money around the school in front of her peers. That's about it."

"What do you mean by *'flaunting her money around'*?"

He then informed me of something I hadn't thought of before. He told me the Cooks were a fairly well-off family. I knew I should have come to that conclusion myself after seeing the expensive suit Chief Cook was wearing when I met him.

I opened my ears and gave my brother a chance to give me a psychology and economy lesson on money and high school students. "You need to understand, Josh, there are only two things a teenager needs to become popular in high school fast: looks and money. Melanie Cook had both. Although lately, she had more money than she did in the past."

When I asked him for an explanation, he told me that even though Catholic schools have uniforms, the students still find ways to be fashionable. Paying attention to the student's wardrobe wasn't high on my brother's list of things to notice or even discipline students over. However, when the primary subject of conversation in the teacher's lounge happens to be Melanie Cook, and how she had recently started coming to school each day with a different pair of shoes or some sort of fancy jewelry, he starts to pay attention.

I thought for sure he was going to tell me a story about how he hit up The Cook's for a donation. Instead, he told me how he believed

Melanie had simply taken advantage of the fact that she had turned 18 and applied for a couple of credit cards. That now I had him wondering if one of his students may have been selling drugs on the side.

I tried to put my younger brother's mind at ease. "Don't let it stress you out too much, Jacob. Remember, this is my case, not yours. Your job is to help people get to Heaven. My job is to help the police department get a murderer."

He agreed. "Well, Josh, I need to get ready for Mass. Will you do me a favor?" He paused and cleared his throat before asking me, "Will you please keep me posted on your progress?"

I had never made a promise to my family I wasn't willing to keep, and I wasn't going to break this one. So, my last words to him before I left the confessional were the very same words that I had said to every priest who had ever heard my Confession, "Will do, Father, will do."

Chapter 8

The four o'clock Mass ended fifteen minutes before five. That was part of the reason why my brother was so popular; he kept his homily short and to the point. He knew how to make people feel good about themselves in just a few simple sentences. Even the most controversial of Gospel passages, like where Jesus talks about divorce. My brother could find some sort of way to water it down and make people feel good about it. He was so good at it; he could sugarcoat death. He would be the perfect priest to do Melanie's funeral, if the Cooks would have him do it. I thought about mentioning it to Chief Cook once I arrived at his house, but then I thought it wouldn't be appropriate to talk about his daughter's funeral as I was searching through her room looking for answers.

Grief hits people in different ways. Chief Cook wanted answers, and I knew he wouldn't mourn until he had them. I had known about the five stages of grief for years. He jumped right to anger. I was willing to bet whatever stage of grief other people close to Melanie were going to jump to was going to be different.

I meditated on these things during my drive to the Cook residence until I arrived. I pulled in the driveway five minutes after five. My brother was right; the Cooks were loaded. The Cook family lived in an extremely nice subdivision just past the corner of Perryville Road and Riverside Boulevard. It was a busy but not too busy intersection on the north side of town, on the nicer side of Rockford. Their home was a minute away from Interstate Ninety, a convenient spot to call home in Rockford. Go east, and you'd be in Chicago in under two hours, go west, and you'd be in Wisconsin in twenty minutes. How anyone could live with the highway practically in their backyard is beyond me. But then again, I'm a sixty-five-year-old man living like a millennial in a one-bedroom apartment close to downtown. To each his own, I guess.

The house itself was a two-story monstrosity. It had one of those large clear glass windows on the second floor. You know, the kind where you look through it and all you can see is one of those big and shiny chandeliers? Yeah, they had one of those too. The sides of the house were completely brick. The front of the house had white aluminum siding that outlined the oversized window. The front porch was solid brown oakwood, and the dark green front door added the finishing touches to the structure. What more can I say, after being at the church, it was apparently a great day for me to look at horrible examples of interior decorating and architecture.

The dark green door swung open before I could ring the doorbell.

"You're late!" Chief Cook said straight into my nose. Although he was shorter than me, that didn't stop him from acting like a bigger man.

"Sorry," I told him. "I was attending Mass like a good little Catholic boy."

He took a few steps back into his home before asking me, "Oh, how is your brother?"

"He's doing well," I said as I removed the tan-colored porkpie hat from my head. "Should I take off my shoes?" I asked before entering his house any further.

]"I prefer that you did," he snapped back at me before walking towards the kitchen.

I followed him, shutting the front door behind me. We walked down a hallway with a hardwood floor that led from the front door into the kitchen. The family room, the stairs leading up to the second floor, and the bedrooms were all carpeted from what I could see. The carpeting in the family room and on the stairs was a light lavender color. I could tell his wife had most likely been the one who picked it out.

He invited me to sit down at the large wooden kitchen table and he even offered me a drink.

I had the urge to ask for something alcoholic, but figured since I was technically on duty, asking for alcohol would not be the best choice. So, I told him I would just that whatever they had in the fridge. It didn't stop him from giving me a laundry list of everything they had. When he finally named off a dark soda with sugar and caffeine in it, I stopped him and said, "I'll take that."

He turned around and raised an eyebrow to the ceiling. "Are you sure you don't want me to mix it with something?" He showed me a bottle of cognac he kept inside his refrigerator.

"I only drink that stuff straight," I told him before reminding him I was on duty.

"I see," was the only thing he had to say. He held onto the bottle in his left hand and grabbed some ice cubes from the freezer with his right. He used his elbow to close the freezer door. Then he put the bottle of cognac down on the counter before reaching up to pull a glass from the cabinet above his head.

I reminded him of the fact I only drink that stuff straight.

"So, no ice?"

I thought about it for a split second before finally giving in and telling him ice was fine.

He shoved the ice into the glass and poured the light brown liquid on top of it before sliding it over to me.

In one swift solid motion, I stood up halfway out of my chair, grabbed the glass as it was still sliding, lifted it up, put it to my lips, and downed the whole thing. I slid the glass back to him.

He was a little perplexed. He poured me some more and told me, "I would prefer it if you slowed down a bit. Keep in mind, you are on duty," he reminded me.

"What do you think I did all the time while I was on duty?"

He twitched his mouth a bit before pouring a glass for himself. Once he finished pouring his glass, he put the bottle back in the fridge before sitting down next to me.

I couldn't think of anything to say, so I started the conversation with some small talk about his kitchen table and I asked him if he built it himself.

"Yep," he took a sip of his drink, "and the chairs too." He took another sip before telling me a story about how he told his wife when they bought the place that he didn't want it to be filled with all kinds of cute girly stuff. I could relate. After all, a man's home is his castle, and in order for a home to feel like a home, some men need to have something in it that was built by their own two hands. In this case, that thing was a large thick wooden table.

I continued to listen to his story about how it would take more than an ax to put a crack through the thing he created and how many men it would take just to carry it out of his house. As he rambled on, I kept right on drinking.

I was about to finish before he reached over the table and grabbed my wrist. "Look, Slim, let's cut the small talk. You're here to do a job, and I'm here to make sure you do it right."

He was a little bit on edge about me being here, as he should be. After all, I was about to search through his daughter's room to see what this young buck missed. He reminded me that his wife would be home soon, and I needed to act fast. He told me that if I thought he was on edge about me being there, his wife was going to be even more so. She knew he never invited people from work over at all. He had told her a little white lie about how today was my last day on the force, and since I was one of his best men, he wanted to make me feel like the two of us could be friends now. Then he asked me if I was willing to play along with his little game, and if I understood everything he said.

I told him I understood. Then, I finished my drink and told him I was ready to rock and roll.

We walked up the light lavender carpet covered stairs and into a hallway of white painted walls with nothing on them. The hallway was bare, but his daughter's room wasn't.

It was neat, organized, and clean, which was a surprise to me. When my brother and I were teenagers, our rooms were filthy. There was one corner of the room near the closet where a giant junk pile seemed to have been growing with each passing day.

"Nice room," I said as I headed inside the enclosed space.

He agreed before going on a rant about how Melanie always kept her room that way.

I asked if the junk pile was his doing.

He said, "No," and told me he had left it alone on purpose for me to sort through.

"I can tell," I said while I stared down at the mess pile on the floor.

I glanced around and found it strange how there were no pictures of anything on the walls. No posters of boy bands, no photographs of friends or family, and no cute little inspirational quotes or sayings anywhere. I always thought teens decorated their rooms as a way of expressing themselves and their interests to everyone who entered their domain.

"You haven't seen her walk-in closet," Chief Cook reminded me, noticing my glances at the walls before he pointed to the closet door.

I walked towards the closet. The outside of the closet door was pure, untouched by anything, including scotch tape. I couldn't see a single mark on the wood, but when I opened it, the inside of the door had all sorts of pictures of her friends from various, past and present high school events: Cheerleading, dances, and other school-related events, hanging from it.

The chief asked if I was surprised by what I saw.

"No, but I'm surprised teenagers nowadays know what photographs are."

He shrugged his shoulders and gave me his thoughts on the subject. He told me how the kids nowadays take pictures with their phones and then take them down to the store. They use a USB cord to plug their device into a computer of sorts and get the pictures printed that way. He and I both still remembered the days when digital cameras weren't that great, and the majority of people were still using thirty-five-millimeter film.

"I remember the days when people only used thirty-five-millimeter," I said aloud, acknowledging my age as I proceeded to walk into the junkyard that was Melanie's closet.

One bare wall of her closet was covered in pictures of good and happy times with family members and friends. In the center of the wall was an inspirational quote about loving yourself and others. I couldn't help but wonder; why would a teenage girl hide all of the things that bring out the best in her on the walls inside her closet?

I turned then to look at the bookshelf that reached almost to the top of the ceiling. The top shelf was full of grade school, middle school, and high school yearbooks. The bottom shelves near toward the floor were filled with childhood knickknacks. Items like tiny stuffed toy teddy bears and miniature figurines were on those lower shelves. They were organized in a manner where they could be beautifully displayed without collecting a large amount of dust. The shelves that would have been eye-to-stomach level for Melanie were the ones that interested me the most. They were filled with books on video recording and making movies.

"Interesting books," I told the girl's father.

His eyes filled up with water, and his smile filled up with teeth. "That was Melanie's dream. She wanted to direct her own movie one day."

I had to know, so I asked, "What did you think about her dream?"

He thought she was just being a typical teenager. Head in the clouds and reaching for the stars. His wife was the one who encouraged her to go for it. Heck, his wife even helped Melanie start her own channel and post videos online. She called it *"Melanie Sings"*. It really wasn't anything at all. It was just his daughter singing her favorite songs, acapella. None of her videos got a whole lot of views or comments, he told me. The only people who'd watch them were relatives and friends. His smile diminished, and the tears ran down his cheeks.

I guess it finally hit him that those little videos his daughter made, the ones he had once thought ridiculous and a waste of time, were now the most valuable and cherished things to him on the Internet.

I turned away to let him shed a few tears without me seeing. I inspected the clothes in Melanie's closet by moving each hanger one at a time to see the type of outfits she wore. I couldn't help but notice her fancier dresses (especially the ones that would have exposed cleavage and a whole lot of leg), were the ones she hung up on the most expensive hangers she owned. The hangers were solid wood except for the metal hook that could be placed on the rack. The dresses were hung up neatly and with extreme care. A clear plastic bag from the dry-cleaners must have been replaced over them time and time again to keep them clean and intact.

There were two dresses in the front of the rack that caught my eye. One was solid black and the other was solid red. The four other dresses behind those two were also skimpy, but instead of being of solid colors, they had bright colors and unique patterns. The rest of the clothes in her closet were ones she wore every day, and the uniforms she wore to school. Those were hung on plastic hangers and they weren't hung up as neatly as her dresses were. Instead, it was almost as if she just threw them on hangers just to get them out of the way.

I looked again at the wall with the photographs again and asked her father, "Don't you find it strange that all of her most precious pictures and all of her most prized possessions are stuffed into the closet while the rest of her room is almost completely bare?"

"Not really," he said before he gave me the logical conclusion he had come to, how Melanie's closet has always been her hiding spot. It had always been her secret place, her sacred hideaway. Whenever she was sad or something upset her, she would run into her closet and lock the door. He started tearing up again.

He went into a story about how he even remembered this one time when Melanie was younger. She was so upset, and she had locked herself in her closet for so long, that he and his wife proceeded to do everything in their power to try and get her to come out sooner. They yelled at her. They promised they would buy her all kinds of things. They even told her when dinner was ready, the typical parent reactions. When she didn't come down, they put a plate next to the closet door just to see if she would open it. She didn't come out that night until they were both in bed. He said they must have been asleep for only an hour before Melanie came to their room and asked if she could have dinner now. He admitted that he had wanted to spank her. But his wife, reacting quicker than him, threw her arms around the little girl before taking her downstairs, making her whatever she wanted to eat. As soon as he finished telling me the story, the tough guy turned away and went out of the room so I wouldn't see him cry.

While he was out of the room and out of my sight, composing himself, I scanned the entire closet with my eyes. I couldn't find any sort of diary or journal, but then again, teenagers rarely use those anymore. Instead, they write on blogs or post things to social media. The only other items I found on the closet floor, other than her pile of material possessions, were a blanket and a fluffy pillow. The chief was right about Melanie making her closet her own little personal getaway from the world. Finding nothing else to discover, I walked out of the closet and looked at the dresser with a large mirror on it that was to my left. I placed one hand on one of the handles of the dresser drawer, preparing to open it.

Cook walked back in and stopped me before I could. "You don't have to look in there, Slim. I've already searched those drawers. I figured I'd save you the trouble. That's where my daughter kept her more intimate belongings. If you know what I mean."

I knew what he meant, and I respected the man's wishes. After all, if I was in his shoes, I wouldn't want some old fart like me or one even close to my age going through my daughter's panty drawer. I decided not to push the issue, and instead, I complimented the chief on how well his daughter's bed was made.

"What do you mean by that?" he asked in a defensive manner.

Not wanting him to think I was implying anything I replied, "Well, I don't know about you, but I'm pretty confident a vast majority of teenagers don't make their beds in the morning."

As soon as he realized I didn't mean anything sick or sinister by it, he cooled his jets and told me it was a habit Melanie had recently formed. Apparently, she had told her father a story about watching a video on the routines successful people have every day. The first habit they mentioned was to make your bed every morning before you do anything else.

"No wonder I'm not successful," I said before I pulled out a small object from my trench coat pocket.

"What's that?" the homeowner asked out of curiosity.

"It's a mini high-powered flashlight." I showed it to him. I told him I saw it on one of those late-night infomercials and decided to get it. I figured it would come in handy someday and today was the day I was going to use it. Excited about using my new toy, I knelt down on the carpeting and shined it underneath Melanie's bed. She had a few objects stuffed underneath the bed. "Well," I said to the victim's father, "the top of your daughter's bed is immaculate, but underneath is a complete disaster zone."

He told me he had noticed that too, but he wanted to wait for my arrival instead of going through it himself.

I pulled out the objects one-by-one, so he could see them. The first one was Melanie's school backpack. The second object was a tripod with a set of small lights attached to it. I looked back at the bookshelf in the girl's closet. "Looks like she took her hobby a lot more serious than you and your wife ever thought. That's why I love bookshelves. You can always tell a person's interests by what they read."

"If that's the case, I'd hate to see what's on your bookshelf."

I broke the news to him about how I sold most of my books for drinking money. The only books I had left in my apartment were the textbooks I used for teaching Confirmation class at my brother's parish. Also, not forgetting the Bible my brother had given me for my fortieth birthday.

He found my statement surprising. At first, he was surprised how an old guy like me with all this spare time on his hands didn't read, and then he was surprised by how someone would let a guy like me teach a subject like Confirmation.

"I use the library once a month," I mentioned as I continued to wave the flashlight under the bed. "The last book I read was called *'The Goliath Bone'*. It was really good."

"What was it about?"

I didn't want to tell him, but I knew I had to. "It's about these two young adults who are trying to hide a precious artifact, and they get an old beat-up private eye to help them."

He almost laughed. He figured a private eye novel would be the last thing a guy like me would read. He ragged on me a little about how I was taking my hobby a little too seriously, much like his daughter did hers.

I ignored his comments. In any other situation, I would've said something back at him. However, my head was currently stuck under a bed. Then, my flashlight found an object that was wedged between the upper left leg of the bed frame and the wall. It was a flat black object that the chief would have been able to find had he paid more attention to what was underneath his daughter's bed than the mess he chose to ignore. I tried to reach for it but I couldn't. Letting the chief know I had found something, I let out a simple, "Bingo, there it is."

"There what is?" he asked before he got down on his knees to try to see what I had found.

I prevented him from doing so and wiggled my way out from underneath the bed before giving him orders. "Here, help me move this."

We pulled the queen-size bed away from the wall.

I shined my flashlight on the object that had been wedged between the bedframe and the wall. "Jackpot," I said before I picked up what I had spotted thanks to the small ball of light I shined under the bed.

"Melanie's laptop," her dad said while pointing to object in my hand.

I nodded. I was one-hundred percent certain this was going to have something on it that would give us a clue as to who murdered Melanie. I told the chief I knew of a guy who would be able to hack into the laptop without any problems. Once he did, I was sure as shit we would have everything we needed to track down Melanie's killer.

"Wait a minute, Slim," he said, stretching his hand out as if to take the laptop away from me. "Shouldn't we take this down to the station? I mean, I've got some computer experts in the department who could hack into that thing probably easier and quicker than your man could."

I couldn't let the chief have the laptop. He was still a suspect in the case of his daughter's murder. If the laptop was taken to the station, who wasn't to say he would be looking over someone's shoulders and having them erase incriminating evidence? I couldn't directly say what was going through my mind to his face. So, I went about my case for keeping the laptop a different way. "You may be right, Chief, but let me ask you this, do you really want all of your daughter's private and personal information floating around the station?"

After a moment he saw my point and agreed to let me have it.

"Thank you," I said before I mentioned how I was going to take the laptop to my car. Not just so I knew it would be safe, but so I also knew if he changed his mind, he wouldn't be able to take it from me unless he wrestled my car keys away from me.

He prevented me from leaving the room, but only for a few seconds, and he did so with his words and not by physical force. He tried to get the words he was trying to say out of his mouth for a moment, but they wouldn't budge. Then, he bobbed his head back-and-forth before he finally looked me directly in the eye and forcing out what he wanted to say. "Look, I don't know you all that well. I don't know Daniel's that well either, but I do know a lot of people in the department that know you well, and they trust you. I also know there is no point in arguing with Carlson on anything. He's like a lawyer with a badge. But if all these people trust you, then so do I. I am glad you are on this case, and I really do appreciate everything that you're doing for me and the department."

I didn't know what to think. I didn't know if he was just trying to butter me up or if he really was giving me a sincere thank you. All I said was, "You're welcome, Chief."

I had just made it out of Melanie's room and almost made it to the stairs when he started talking to me again. He started to tell me about how he had pulled my record up, and then went on a tangent about how the work I did with the department impressed him. Having only one unsolved case during my thirty years of service was impressive. Then, he started to talk about something I had hoped he wouldn't. "You didn't have to retire just because you had one unsolved case. I mean, what happened in Beloit…"

"Chief," I interrupted him. "We don't talk about what happened in Beloit." I walked downstairs, put my shoes on, and walked out the door.

It was still raining when I got to my car. I opened my driver's side door and took a moment to see where the best place for me to hide the laptop would be. I ducked down and placed the laptop on the floor of the passenger side. I then took the towel located on the passenger seat and threw that on top of it. I kept a towel on the passenger seat because well, I'm a guy and I like to eat in my car. It was the only way I could think of how to prevent the grease from the fast-food bags, wrappers, and the food itself from getting on the seat of my car.

No sooner than I got the laptop covered did I hear a voice from behind me say, "Oh, you must be Josh."

I climbed slowly out of my car to see another vehicle beside mine with a woman sitting inside it. It was larger than a compact vehicle, looked similar to an SUV, but different in many ways.

She introduced herself to me through the rolled-down passenger side window of the large, gray vehicle. "I'm Jennifer Cook. Pete's wife."

Chapter 9

She reminded me of one of those actresses from the old black and white film noir movies. Her blonde hair went from the top of her head to just a little ways past her shoulders. The rain seemed to slide off her hair like it was one big blonde waterslide. She was slightly taller than the chief and a little bit older too. My guess was somewhere between ten and fifteen years. She wore a navy-blue coat that was more suitable for winter than it was in the rain, but it matched her eyes, so I couldn't really blame her for wearing it.

Once she got out of her car, I saw that her jacket was open. She was wearing a white blouse, and thanks to the rain, I could see everything underneath it. Her black skirt just barely touched her kneecaps. Where it ended, her black diamond-pattern stockings continued, going past the buckles of her black shoes. Once my eyes hit the ground, they flew right back up like bouncy balls to her all-natural no makeup covered face.

She spoke, "I don't know if you were able to hear me through the window, but I'm Pete's wife, Jennifer." She smiled. Her teeth matched her blouse.

It took a second for me to shake myself out of the funk. "Pete? Oh, yes, Chief Cook. I forgot Peter was his first name."

"Most people do," she said as she shot me a quick smile before clicking a button on a small remote that she held in her hand. The trunk of her car popped up in the air, and that wasn't the only thing popping up. She grabbed a bag of groceries from the trunk and put it in front of her, blocking my view of the beauty that was her chest. "I've got two more bags in the trunk. You don't mind helping me carry them inside, do you?"

I blinked for a second. "Sure, sure," I said before grabbing the two bags, each one probably twice as heavy as the one she was carrying.

She closed the trunk of the car with her right hand and held it there for a moment as if to show off her Pandora bracelet with the various charms on it. Either that or she was showing me her lavender-painted fingernails, which matched the carpeting in her house perfectly. Her ring finger was painted white, like the walls in Melanie's room.

"You got it?" she asked.

It took me a second to bring my mind back to the groceries. "Yeah," I told her. "I'm just not used to having this much food in my arms."

A tiny giggle left her mouth. "You make it so obvious that you are a bachelor, detective." She held her hand up in the air once again and pressed a button to lock her car.

I followed the moving pair of diamond-patterned stockings up to the green door. As soon as those little black shoes of hers touched the front porch, the green door opened and Chief Cook greeted his wife. "Here, honey, let me get that for you," he said before taking the grocery bag out of her hand. After she was inside the house, the homeowner turned around and greeted me. "Hey, Slim, perfect timing. Well, I see you found the place without any problem. Come on in."

This was the game he was talking about earlier. I knew it all too well, so I decided to ham it up a bit. "Thanks for having me over, Chief. Did you want me to take off my shoes?"

He gave me a small grin. "If you don't mind."

I kicked off my shoes and carried the two big bags of groceries into the kitchen, where Mrs. Jennifer Cook instructed me to put them down on the counter next to the sink. I got a good look at her left hand. Her diamond ring wasn't anything glamorous, but if I pawned it, it would have been enough for me to buy everyone at Carl's a round of drinks or two. Even on a packed Saturday night.

"So, Josh," she interrupted my train of thought, "tell me, if you were to describe retirement in one word, what would it be?"

"Boring!"

The chief shot me a look as if I had given the wrong answer to a question on a game show and just caused our team to lose. It was clear I had given the wrong answer, but it was the only answer I could think of.

Mrs. Cook gave a fake laugh to my answer. "Boring? How is it boring? You've only been retired for an hour," she said, continuing the conversation. I continued to watch her as she took off the navy-blue coat she was wearing and tossed it on the kitchen counter. It didn't stay there for long as it slid off, landing somewhere between the head of the table and the end of the patio doors. It was kind of nice to see a woman as beautiful as her throwing her clothes around and letting them land anywhere on the floor.

"What can I say? I like to keep busy, and for the past hour, I haven't been all that busy, Mrs. Cook." I responded as I looked at the black business sport coat that had been underneath that navy-blue jacket.

"Please call me Jennifer." She quickly buttoned up the sport coat in an attempt to keep herself modest in front of her house guest.

"Sure," I said hesitating for a moment before practically stuttering her name, "Jennniiiffeeer."

This time, she gave me a real laugh. "Oh, you're so old-fashioned and formal. I love it." As she began pulling the groceries out of the bags, she instructed the two of us to sit down at the kitchen table.

The chief saw the two glasses of cognac still sitting on the table. He quickly grabbed mine and put it behind a plant that was sitting on an end table next to the patio doors. "Would you like something to drink, Slim?"

I smiled. "I'll have whatever you're having." I winked at him and pointed to his glass, which was still on the table, for all to see. He smirked before rising from the chair.

I don't know if he kept giving me that face because he didn't like my answers or because I was consuming all of his cognac.

"So, Josh," Jennifer asked as she ran those jewelry-covered hands of hers under running water, "Why does everybody call you 'Slim'?".

I leaned back in the chair and smiled as I waited for my next drink to arrive. "That's my last name. My full name is Joshua Nathan Slim."

She stopped what she was doing and removed her hands from the running water. "Are you by any chance related to Father Slim?"

"Yes, I am," I said proudly. "And his full name is Jacob Michael Slim."

"I thought so," she said waving one of those long fingers of hers at me. "Our daughter Melanie goes to his school, right, Pete?"

Chief Cook fiddled around in the refrigerator and ignored his wife while she talked to him.

"Speaking of Melanie, I haven't seen her since she went out last night. Have you seen her at all today, Pete?"

"No. I have not," Cook said, closing the refrigerator door and bringing the drink over to me rather than sliding it over to me like he had the last time. "I better go get the grill started."

Chief Cook practically ran out onto the deck to fire up the grill. The only thing stopping him was the patio door. He slid it open as fast as he could.

I stood and shut it gently, so Jennifer and I could talk in private.

After a moment of silence between the two of us, she broke the long, quiet pause between us by saying, "So, thirty years with the same police department."

"Yep," I said, raising my glass to her before turning it to my lips.

"I can't imagine being at the same job for thirty years. What made you decide you wanted to become a cop?"

Rather than give her my full life story, I gave her my earliest recollection. "I broke up a fight between two seniors when I was a freshman in high school."

She let out another one of her fake laughs. "I bet those boys were embarrassed."

"Not really. In fact, they pinned the whole thing on me."

"The principal didn't believe you?"

"Two senior boys against the word of a freshman. It was my word against theirs."

"What happened after that?"

"The principal gave me a three-day suspension. My mom and dad told me I couldn't leave the room during those three days, except to go to the bathroom."

"What did your brother say about the whole ordeal?"

I rolled my eyes and head. I didn't want to go into what that self-righteous momma's boy said, but I knew I had to. "He said, 'Blessed are the peacemakers; for they shall be called the children of God.' It wasn't very helpful to my situation, but he was the only one who believed me."

"So, you broke up a fight, and that was the event in your life that made you want to become a cop?"

"No. It was the way I was treated after the fact." I found myself making the same face her husband had made at me. "After that day, I swore justice would be done no matter where I went. I would be the voice of the little guy, and every little guy would have a voice with me."

Immediately after I finished talking, the patio door opened. "Hey, Slim!" the chief now turned chef heating up the grill shouted. "Quit yacking with my wife and bring me the meat! The grill is almost six-hundred degrees."

Jennifer rose and quickly slapped the steaks on a plate and sent me outside with it. She shut the patio doors behind me once I was.

No sooner had my host thrown the steaks on the grill did he ask me, "So, what are you and Jennifer talking about in there?"

"Just small talk about how and why I chose law enforcement as an occupation," I said before adding in, "Speaking of which, we never really discussed my pay for…"

"You'll get whatever your salary was before you quit!" He interrupted me. "Solve it before Tuesday morning, and I'll give you a full week's worth of pay."

"Why Tuesday morning?"

He was getting pissy from my line of questions. "How stupid do you think people are? You heard my wife in there. Melanie has been missing for almost a full day now. If she's not home by Sunday night, Jennifer will have a panic attack. Melanie not being in school for a day is one thing, but her not being on her phone for four days is another. You know how these kids are nowadays. Their phones are glued to their fingers. They are on them twenty-four-seven. If Melanie doesn't post something on at least one of her social media accounts every day, people will think she fell off the face of the earth." He turned around to look at the steak. "I can't keep my daughter in the morgue forever, Slim. I will have to bury her by this time next week."

I put my hand on his shoulder. "I'll find the son-of-a-bitch, sir. I promise I will."

The patio door opened, and the lady of the house shouted, "Hey, how many men does it take to cook a steak! Just so you two know, I like my steak medium, not well done."

My host continued to play with the meat on the grill. I stood nearby, watching with little-to-no interest in his grill methods. Once the steaks were done, he placed them on the plate I was holding. After doing so, we both walked back into the kitchen and sat down for dinner.

I decided to open the conversation. "So, Jennifer, since you asked questions about me, I figured I should ask a few questions about you. How long have you been a, uh…um…" Forgetting if I even knew her occupation.

"An accountant?" she finished my sentence for me, so I wouldn't be embarrassed any more than I already was. She started to tell me how she had been in the field for sixteen years; but then she seemed to change her story slightly by telling me she had only been at her current firm for five.

Once I understood what she was trying to tell me, I asked her what made her decide to become an accountant.

She fumbled with the condiments on the table before answering my question. She told me she went back to school after Melanie was born. She figured if she was going to finish her degree, the perfect time to do so was when Melanie was still a baby.

"Interesting," I commented as I did the math in my head to figure out if she was lying to me or not. Before I started carrying numbers in my head, I asked her, "But, why accounting?"

She gave me a smile that seemed as fake as the laughs she had previously given me. She then went into a speech that almost seemed rehearsed. With confidence in her voice, she told me how she had loved math ever since she was a kid, and how she had always gotten A's in the subject.

"I've always said the three things I'm good at are math, money, and men," she said before she shot me a smile and proceeded to touch her husband's shoulder. It was as if the comment was some sort of joke that allowed her to show off her husband to the world.

I decided to shift the conversation from focusing on her to the two of them, and asked them how they met.

Jennifer looked at her man as though she was waiting for him to tell the story, but he kept right on chewing his food. So, she decided to tell it instead. She went on to tell me that before she met Pete, she'd been married to a man who was a hyper-masculine control freak. The type that firmly believed women should do nothing but stay home to make babies and dinner. It took her a while, but she eventually managed to build up the courage to leave him. Then one night, after the two of them had already split the legal way, her ex-husband showed up at the doorstep ready to attack her, but the chief, who was only a beat cop at the time, came to her rescue. He was her knight-in-shining-armor, and she concluded the story by telling me about how he still was, to this day. She continued to touch him, brushing her hand up and down his arm.

My host's cell phone let off a loud buzzing sound. He looked at it for a moment before informing the two of us that he had to take the call.

Once he was out of the room, I did my best to brag about him to his wife. "Your husband is a wonderful man and a great boss too, Jennifer. Why today, he…"

"Shut up," she said, interrupting me.

"Excuse me?" I asked, confused as to why she would cut me off so fast. The thought crossed my mind that either she was bi-polar or everything she just said had been one big act.

She flipped her hair back, which gave me a better look at her pale white face, which was starting to turn pink. "I don't know why you are here, Slim, but I will tell you this. Pete has never once brought a co-worker into this house. I don't care how good of a guy you are or how many years you've put in for the department. I believe you are here for one reason, and one reason only: Something has happened to my Melanie. Now, I don't know what's going on, but if you find my daughter, I'll give you whatever you want."

She used her right hand to unbutton the top two buttons of the slow-drying white blouse she had been wearing underneath the black sport coat. She flashed a part of her white bra at me. Then she put four of her fingers into the cup, fully intending on showing me what was underneath the white undergarment. Before she could, however, her husband walked back into the kitchen.

"Hey, Slim, can I see you for a moment?" he yelled from the edge of the kitchen, not even noticing his wife almost flashing me.

I got up out of my chair and stood in front of her for a second. Giving her the option to finish what she started or to cover herself. I'm sad to say she chose the second option. I walked over to my boss and asked him, "What's up?"

He led me back outside to the patio. Sickler had called him, and the two of them had been talking while Jennifer and I had been talking at the table. *And doing her best to bribe me,* I thought to myself. The chief gave me a quick explanation about how Sickler's daughter was friends on Facebook with Melanie. Sickler was using her daughter's phone to look at

Melanie's social media accounts. Apparently, one of Melanie's friends had made a few posts asking Melanie questions like, "Where are you? What are you doing? Why aren't you answering your phone?" A few of her classmates had commented on the post as well, and a few even liked them. People were starting to get suspicious, and he wasn't liking it.

I asked him what he wanted me to do about it.

"Solve this case," was the response he gave me. His index finger hit the center of my chest.

After reminding me I had Melanie's laptop in my car, he told me to see what I could find on there. If my computer guy was as good as I claimed him to be, I should also have him get on Melanie's Facebook and make some kind of post to avoid anyone else becoming concerned. Then, he asked me to use my brother's vice-principal power to get me inside the school so that I could look around there tomorrow morning. Giving me the chance see if there were any clues in Melanie's locker.

I thought about that for a moment, and hoped that whatever was found on the laptop would be conclusive enough for me to avoid having to go to the school. Dealing with a place usually filled by teens with attitude problems and whatever they hid at school from their parents, was the last thing I wanted to put on my To-Do list.

Chief Cook ended his rant by throwing the reputation I had built up for myself in my face and reminding me how he wasn't paying me in food and cognac. This quickly stopped me from thinking about how to get out of investigating the high school.

"Speaking of which, how do you intend to pay me for this job?" I asked him bluntly.

The question led to a cold stare between our two hotheads. Our staring contest was broken up by Jennifer when she peaked her head out the patio door and said, "Boys, the rest of the food is getting cold. You two can talk business later."

We went back to the kitchen. Before my host took his seat, he turned back around to look into his living room, noticing something he had been oblivious to until now. Then his head flipped back around to ask Jennifer a question. "Uh, honey, where did the glass coffee table go? You know, the one that was in the living room?"

She took a second to chew on an ice cube in her mouth before answering. "I set it outside where the garbage cans are. You know, on the side of the garage."

He started to turn the same color she was before I left the table. "What happened to the coffee table last night, honey?"

She took a quick swig of her drink. The large ice cube floating at the top of her glass made its way into her mouth. She rolled it around like a piece of hard candy once or twice before answering her husband. "Well, the glass broke last night, so I cleaned up the mess and hauled the thing outside."

"Why didn't you tell me about it earlier?"

Her teeth cracked down on the piece of frozen water. After the bits of ice slid down that sexy throat of hers, she explained to him how she really didn't have an opportunity to do so last night. After the chief had finished with his latest hobby, he had given her a call to let her know that something horrible had happened down at the station. It was clear he hadn't told her what.

She went on to say how she had woken up this morning by herself, and he hadn't gotten home until she was about to leave for work. Then, she didn't hear from him for the rest of the day until he sent her a text, letting her know they would be having a dinner guest tonight.

I love how couples fight in front of company. They try to be all cool and calm about the things bothering them, but their grinding teeth, phony smiles, and short sharp sentences show just how much they want to wring the other's neck.

Rather than allow the couple to continue bickering, I decided to interrupt their feud with a question. "Speaking of last night, Chief, where were you between the hours of nine and ten? We tried calling your cell phone multiple times, but we just couldn't get ahold of you."

He gave me the same grin he had been giving his wife the entire time. He clearly wanted to keep quiet about something, but he wouldn't say what it was.

Fortunately, Jennifer knew exactly what he wasn't telling me. "Pete is in a band," she said with enthusiasm. "They get together every Friday night for practice."

"I see," I said, barely believing his story. "Are you guys any good?"

"We, uh, haven't played anywhere yet," he said while he cut the remainder of his steak into smaller pieces than it already was. "There are a lot of kinks we need to work out before we perform in front of a live audience."

"I see," I said once again, before turning my attention towards Jennifer. "Have you heard his band play?"

She looked at him with those piercing eyes of hers before telling me that she had yet to see him play or hear one of the songs the band was working on. Then, she let another ice cube roll into her mouth before she put it between her pearly whites. She pushed it over to the side of her mouth with her wet slippery tongue and crushed it in her mouth, much like the way she wanted to crush him in the arguments they would have after I left.

I still wasn't buying it. "What instrument do you play?"

"Guitar," he said, without so much as looking up at me.

We continued to eat and make small talk about meaningless things such as his band, and the weather, until dinner was eaten, the dishes were done, and I was about to leave.

As we all headed down the hallway to the front door, Chief Cook excused himself for a moment to go to the bathroom, which gave his wife and me an opportunity to talk.

"Do you think the part about the band is true?" I whispered, leaning closer to her.

"I think so," she said, moving her eyes from the hallway to meet mine. "I don't think he would ever cheat on me."

"What makes you say that?"

She gave me a short explanation about something I should have figured out from the start. "Pete is horrible with money. Without me, he would be overdrawn and maxed out before Halloween. Trust me, Pete knows better not to cheat."

"Do you?"

She gave me a sour face, but she quickly changed it the moment her husband came out of the bathroom.

"Well, Slim, are you ready to go?"

"Sure am." I turned away from him to look down at the floor. "Just give me a second here to put my shoes on." Once they were on my feet, I addressed him with a smile. "Say, by the way, since I am retired now, you can call me Josh."

"Alright," he acknowledged.

"And I can call you Pete from now on, right?"

"Sure," he said before giving me that sinister grin of his one last time before I left his house. He gave me a tight, firm handshake before I turned to his wife.

"Goodbye, Josh," she said before giving me a soft hug. Her hands touched my shoulder blades in a friendly manner, and her elbows were out as to make herself appear not too friendly towards me in front of her husband.

I followed suit by gently placing my hands on her shoulder blades as well.

She let go of me with her arms before giving me a gentle push with her white and purple fingernails. "Oh, I almost forgot, you should really take some leftovers home with you. You are a bachelor, after all. Here, come back into the kitchen with me. You don't have to take your shoes off."

I shot a quick smile to the man who had made me take off my shoes each and every time

I had entered his house that evening. Then, I walked back to the kitchen, shoes and all.

She was pulling Tupperware containers from the cabinets as fast as she could when I stepped into the kitchen to join her. She grabbed some food from the leftovers she had already put in the fridge and started shoving them into the containers she had set out on the counter. While she was doing so, she whispered in my ear an order. "You find Melanie. You hear me?" She raised her fist to her mouth and bit the side of her hand before finishing up with the phrase, "And you do it as fast as you can."

I tip the top of my head towards her. "I'll do everything I can," I told her before she handed off a plastic bag that was now holding the plastic containers to me. "Do you have any clue where she may have gone or the last thing she did?"

She shook her head back and forth. "All she told me was that she was going to hang out with a friend."

I needed to know the name of this so-called friend, so I asked her, "Do you have any idea who the friend was?"

She gave me a name I didn't want to hear, "Mia Quarry."

Chapter 10

It was the worst thing she could have possibly said to me. I got back in my car and checked to make sure the laptop was still underneath the towel. It was. I put the thin plastic bag holding the plastic containers of food in the backseat of my car. I couldn't allow anything to spill and damage the precious cargo I was carrying.

I made sure I was well out of sight from their house before I parked my car on the side of the road. "Mia," I said out loud as I sat behind the wheel of my bright blue Buick. "Of all the names she had to tell me, why did she have to say it was Mia."

Maybe there was still a chance that my client wasn't the lead suspect. I looked at the digital clock on my dashboard. It was almost eight, and I had a gas station to get to.

As I was pulling out of the subdivision, I did something illegal in the state of Illinois. I pulled out my cell phone and called my computer guy. "Alex, it's Slim. Are you doing anything important this evening?"

"Right now, I'm working on my fourth bowl of cereal of the day. Why do you ask?"

My eyes made a quick shift to the floor of the passenger side where the towel was. "I need a huge favor. I'm working on a case, and I need your help. I've got a teenager's laptop that I need hacking into tonight. Please, tell me you are available." I waited for him to respond.

A few loud crunching sounds came over the phone before Alex's voice did. "Yeah, I can take a look at it. When will you be over?"

The clock in my car showed it was eight. It was hard for me to believe I had spent the past three hours of my life at the Cook's house. I told Alex I could be over there in an hour or so, but I had to stop at a gas station first.

He proceeded to ask me why it was going to take me an hour and if I really was planning on using the facilities for that long at a filling station.

I didn't want to tell him I had to interrogate someone at a gas station. So, I just agreed to the schmuck's assumption.

Then, he had the nerve to ask me if I could pick up a pizza while I was out. If this was going to be the only form of payment he was going to ask me for while he hacked into Melanie Cook's computer, it seemed fair.

"Yeah, sure, I can bring some over. That way, you can eat something today besides cereal."

"Sounds great. Oh, and, Slim, make sure it's a supreme."

I hung up the phone before he asked me for something else. Besides, it probably wasn't the best idea to talk on a cellphone while getting on the interstate. As I was driving, I couldn't help but think about my old friend Alex. He was a computer genius, but he was also a nut. The man was filthy rich, yet he chose to live in a dump. All sorts of companies all over Illinois wanted him to come work for them, but he refused. Instead, he opened up his own business and made big money designing websites for various customers. He had a shit ton of money too, but he rarely spent a dime of it. He lived in a house on the west side of Rockford, in one of the worst neighborhoods you could have possibly imagined. Before I could go there, I had to make my way back to the gas station just before the bridge.

When I arrived at the gas station, I parked my car in front of the two doors and walked through the double glass doors as if I owned the place. A small bell rang, announcing my arrival.

"Hello," a voice hiding in one of the aisles said to me. I looked down the aisle to see a young man in his mid-twenties with slicked-back brown hair, thick glasses, and a goatee mopping the floor.

"Are you Zach?" I shouted to him. I didn't want to get too close just in case the rainbow-haired ponytail warned him of my visit.

"Who wants to know?" The kid asked. He was paying more attention to the dirt on the floor than he was to the customer in the store.

I held up my badge, but he didn't see it.

Like a good gas station attendant, he continued to pay attention to something else besides the customer talking to him.

After being ignored for so long, I finally said, "Detective Josh Slim, Rockford PD."

He stopped mopping and turned around to get a good look at me. "Am I in some sort of trouble?"

"No," I said before putting my retired police officer's badge that I always carried around with me away. "I'm just looking for some information."

"How can you see something you can only hear?"

Smartass.

He turned back around and continued his mopping.

"Look, kid, I need to ask you some questions about an incident that happened last night."

"Not interested." He stuffed the mop back into the bucket and walked all the way around the store in order to avoid me. He was trying to get back to the door leading to the register that would lock him in his cage.

He wasn't too bright as I knew where he was heading. I beat him to the door and shut it with the back of my hand. He almost ran straight into my beer gut with his flat chest and flabby stomach. I told him he wasn't in any sort of trouble, and all I was there to do was ask him some questions about something that happened last night.

He spat two words back at me, "Forget it," before he walked out of the store.

I knew my dad bod couldn't keep up with the pace his skinny frame was moving, so I walked outside and stood in front of the double doors waiting for him to return.

His was the only car in the parking lot other than mine.

I wasn't outside for more than half a minute before I heard a ding behind me. The sneaky son-of-a-bitch had gone back into the store through the back door. I walked back into the gas station.

The kid was in his cage.

"Look, Zach, will you just answer my questions?"

He sat on the high bar stool hidden behind the counter. The little snot pulled out his cell phone as though he was going to record me.

I walked out of the store, acting as if I had given up and were going to leave. He had picked the wrong guy to play games with.

I moved my car into the carwash and parked it there. I should have thought of that sooner. After all, it was the warmest and driest place in the entire parking lot. A lot of gas stations leave the doors to their carwashes open during the summer months as a way of luring customers into them.

As soon as my car was snug in the small brick shelter, I got out and made my way to the front of the building. I was about twenty-five feet away from the doors when I saw Zach come outside for a cigarette. I guess my mere presence stressed him out, but I was about to stress him out even more.

I took the old .45 out of my coat and fired a bullet at the curved door handle.

It startled the kid, and he dropped his cigarette as he ran for his car. I personally would have run back inside the building, but he probably figured I would have fired another bullet at the door.

Instead, I fooled him and fired another round at the ground. I still, to this day, don't know if I hit him in the foot or not. If I did, it was too dark to see any blood, and if I didn't, I gave him such a scare that he tripped over his own two feet.

When he landed, he started to scream. When I walked over to him, he surrendered, and just like that, he was open to talking to me. The things one has to do to get good customer service these days.

I pulled Zach off the ground and began to yell at him. "Why won't you answer my questions?!"

He said he didn't know. The kid was scared. I had shaken him to his core.

"Tell me about the car that was parked on the bridge last night."

"What car?"

"A girl's body was found in the river last night. Now, I need to know, did you see a car on the bridge? Yes, or no?"

"I did," he said, quivering, "but it was only there for a minute."

"What can you tell me about it?"

He continued to shake, so I took my gun and fired a bullet towards the road, and I promised him I would aim the next one at the pumps and blow us both sky-high.

"It was an SUV, I think. It was only there for a minute. Whoever was their popped open their trunk and that was all I saw."

"What color was the SUV?"

"I don't remember."

I shook him some more.

"You can't legally do this to me!"

I let go of him for a second so I could take the back of my hand and slap him. "I can't legally do that either, but I just did. Now tell me, what color was the SUV you saw last night."

"I swear, I don't remember. I saw a shadow pop open the trunk on the bridge, and that was it. Then I went back to watching YouTube videos on my phone."

I stood up tall and took a few steps away from him.

He did a crabwalk back to his car. He raised his hand and started to play with the door to his car until he realized two things; one, it was locked, and two, I wasn't going to threaten him anymore. In his confusion, he asked me, "Wait, that, was it? That was all you wanted?"

"Yeah, why?'

He started laughing like he was some psychotic clown. "I seriously thought for a moment you were here because," he stopped.

I couldn't let him. "Because of what?" I shouted back at him.

He composed himself before speaking. He started confessing to me about something he and his pals did at this location, including the night Melanie Cook's body had been found. He said that he and his friends had heard a bunch of sirens coming their way. The kids at the gas station figured the cops were on their way here to bust them for all the drugs they had exchanged and been using in his employer's parking lot. Even though the cops went down Route Two, he was still shaken up by the thought of being busted, and that was why he was avoiding me. He said if I had been upfront with him, to begin with, he would have told me about the car.

Of course, it all makes sense because, in today's world of retail, the customer is always wrong.

I asked him to tell me more about the drugs he and his buddies were doing and who they got them from.

He refused.

I pointed my gun at him and threatened to fire it again if he didn't tell me.

He said I didn't have the guts before he informed me there was a hidden camera in the parking lot. A camera didn't stop me from doing what I did the first time, so I asked him to show me where it was. When he pointed to a lamp post close by, I aimed my gun at the thirty-foot object and fired a bullet at it. There was a cute explosion before the light went out, then the kid started talking again. "Okay, okay. I'll tell you. There is this group of guys who come here from Chicago. I think they are in their thirties or something. They are like, really old."

If thirty was old, then I was ancient. I kept my mouth shut.

He kept right on rambling. "Anyway, they come here once a month to meet up with some people from the small towns off of Route Two in our parking lot. They do drug deals right here in the lot, and then they leave."

I started to ask for more information, but two cars pulled into the parking lot distracting the kid. Instead of asking them to call the police or to give him a ride away from me, he said, "I have to go. I have customers." Then he used the darkness to get to the door of the gas station.

I let Zach go back to work. I had the information I wanted. I decided I would forward the tip about the gas station drug deals to

Carlson later on. Having spent enough time weaseling info out of the kid, I looked at my phone to see how long I had stayed. It was a quarter after nine, it had been over an hour, and I knew I still had to pick up a few pizzas before I headed over to Alex's. I just hoped he could find something on Melanie's laptop. Then again, finding information on a teenage girl's computer shouldn't be as hard as finding a late-night pizza place in Rockford, Illinois.

Chapter 11

I showed up at Alex's house with the pizza he requested in hand at ten minutes to ten. I used my foot to kick the door a few times, knowing the doorbell didn't work. I also didn't want to use my hands for anything more than keeping the pizza balanced. When the door opened, there was classic Alex, still in his flannel plaid pajamas, dark blue robe, and tan slippers all of which he had probably been wearing for most of the week. His long brown unwashed hair that went past his shoulders and his beard that covered his entire neck made him look like a hermit who lived in the mountains. Although he didn't smell anything like the outdoors. "Come in, come in," he said before he grabbed the pizza out of my hands. "The food's probably cold by now."

I didn't care to explain to him where I got it from, nor did it matter. It was pizza, and most of the pizza places in Rockford got their boxes from the same distributor. So, unless you were a pizza connoisseur, you would have had no clue which of the twenty-six pizza places in Rockford your pie came from.

As soon as I stepped into Alex's house, I was greeted with a bark from his red-haired poodle, who refused to get off the recliner he was sitting comfortably on. "Hello, Teddy," I said to the dog.

The dog didn't move from the chair. He just sat there and continued to bark at me until his owner started talking again.

"Have a seat, Slim!" Alex shouted at me from the kitchen as he attempted to find something to put our dinner on.

I looked around the junkyard that was his living room. The sixty-inch flat screen smart TV sat on the floor either because he was too lazy or he didn't have the skills to mount it. In front of the television were a collection of monitors, laptops, and computer cords. To the left of the television was Teddy's recliner, and to the left of that was a couch filled with computer books and equipment.

In the middle of the room, closer to the couch, was a coffee table with nothing on it. Rather than ruin the beauty of his coffee table, I decided to move some computer textbooks from the couch onto the floor, so I could have a seat. Alex only possessed the three pieces of furniture. The recliner was Teddy's. The couch functioned as Alex's bed and as a storage facility for papers, books, and equipment he needed for the various projects he was working on. The coffee table functioned as has his desk sometimes, but tonight it was a kitchen table.

"Dinner is served," the hermit said with pride as he brought in two paper plates filled with pizza.

I pulled Melanie's laptop out from behind my back, where I had stuffed it. It had served as a pretty good back brace while I was carrying the pizzas into his bachelor pad. The next time I saw the guys at the bar, I planned to tell them: if they ever needed a back brace and didn't have one, all they had to do was stick a laptop in the waistband of their pants, just above their tailbone.

After I set the rectangle-shaped machine down, I thanked Alex for seeing me at this hour. I also gave a soft apology for interrupting him, which I was sure I wasn't.

Teddy hopped out of his recliner and started to beg for some food while I continued to talk to my computer whiz, hermit friend.

Alex threw a couple of pieces of the pizza away from us to distract his dog so I could hear him over Teddy's whining. "Nonsense," he told me before taking a bite out of the grease-covered food. He started to tell me how he had been working on a project for the city. They wanted him to build a website for the city bus system. They wanted it to have, not only the bus schedules, but also tell you how many minutes until a bus would arrive at a certain location. He was working on an app for them as well.

I didn't give a shit about it or really cared to hear what he had to say, so I just said, "Sounds complicated."

"Not really," he mumbled before he pulled out a few bus schedules that were lodged in between the cushions of the couch. He took another bite of his pizza and continued to talk to me with his mouth full about how they wanted the whole thing done before school started in August but, at the rate he was going, he was going to have everything they wanted, done by the Fourth of July.

"Neat," I said, while not giving a fuck about his project and wondering when he was going to get to mine.

He finally did after he stuffed a full slice of pizza in his mouth and used a blank sheet of computer paper he had laying around as a napkin.

Alex lived the life of a true bum. He was both lazy and cheap. However, when it came to computers, Alex moved like lightning and spared no expense with his work. He sprinted from the couch to grab his own laptop and a few cords. He connected the devices together, turned them both on, and in what I swear was under a minute, he was already hacked into Melanie's laptop. Before the master continued his work, he broke the silence in the room by asking me, "Hey, do you want a drink or something before we get started?"

It took me a second to respond because I was a little shocked by how fast I had just seen him move and by how little effort it took him to get into the device. "I'll take anything you've got in the fridge that's not dairy," I said with the fear in my mind that if he had any milk in the fridge, it had probably expired long ago.

He moved just as fast as he had to get the computers set up and came back into the room with two beers. The beverage brought a smile to my face, and I thanked him before he broke the bad news to me. "You'll never believe it, but the tiny grocery store near your brother's church sells gluten-free beer. That's where I got these. Let me know what you think. I never thought in a million years that someone would develop gluten-free beer."

Gluten-free beer, what kind of sick fuck would make such a thing? I wanted to spit it out and strangle him, but seeing as how he was about to do me a huge favor, I swallowed it and said, "I like the craft stuff better."

"Suit yourself." he said before taking a swig of his. He planted himself back down on the couch and began the work I'd asked him to do. Before looking through Melanie's hacked laptop, he just had to say his personal catchphrase, "Now, let's see what we've got here." After a minute or two of looking it over, he turned his attention towards me. "Uh, Slim, what are we looking for here?"

"The girl who owned this laptop was murdered yesterday. I am trying to find some clue as to who killed her, and why?"

He took a deep breath and gave me some disappointing news. As far as he could tell, Melanie had used her laptop for only four things: School assignments, goofing around on social media, editing pictures, and making videos.

"I doubt any of her school assignments will give me any clue as to how she was murdered. So, let's start by checking her social media," I suggested before eating more pizza to counteract the awful taste of the gluten-free beer.

Melanie had four different social media accounts. We started with the one she used the most. A big blue bar came on the screen, followed by a few notifications and some messages. I looked past all of those things to see a picture of Chief Cook and Jennifer, with Melanie in-between them. They were sitting on a couch in what I remembered as the living room in the Cook family house. There was a glass coffee table in front of them. I could only assume that was the glass coffee table Jennifer told her husband she broke yesterday. To the left of that picture was a picture Melanie had taken of herself with her glasses on. I had no clue until that moment the girl wore glasses.

"Seems she's got some people who are concerned about her." Alex pointed out.

I agreed with him before asking him to scroll down so I could see some of her posts.

He did as I asked, but he seemed more disappointed than I did with the results. "It looks like she's a typical teenage girl to me. All she does is post pictures of herself with her friends and share goofy memes. I wouldn't consider any of this out of the ordinary."

"Well, that's why we are doing this. We need to find things that are out of the ordinary. Let's take a look at one of her other social media accounts. Maybe we can find something there."

I asked Alex to get off of the Book of Faces, and he did so, after rolling his eyes at me calling the website by a different name. He opened another tab then continued to make his way through her browser history to see what other websites Melanie had been active on.

After ten seconds of scrolling, he pointed to the name of a site and said, "Let's try this one." As we waited for the site to load, Alex braced me for disappointment. "I am not so sure about this one, Slim. I don't know too many high schoolers who use this particular social media platform." The social media site he had clicked was called Twitter and its logo was a cute little blue-colored bird. Alex started to tell me how most of the people he knew who use the site were anti-social, divorced, young adults in their twenties and thirties. Most had no money and nothing better to do on a Friday night than play hashtag games.

I wanted to look at him and tell him that the pot was calling the kettle black, but I knew he wouldn't understand the reference. I wasn't going to judge Alex for his choice of lifestyle. I knew if I did, he would throw the laptop back at me and tell me to get out. Even though he was a hermit, Alex was an overly sensitive guy. He didn't like it when people told him how to live his life, which was one of the reasons he usually broke up with a girl the moment she critiqued his life in the slightest bit. So, I just sat there and drank my nasty-ass beer while waiting for the page to load.

It eventually did. At first glance, it seemed similar to the last social media account we looked at. There was a picture of Melanie she had taken of herself. She was wearing her glasses and smiling. Her bright blonde hair was completely down, and only the white wall of her bedroom could be seen behind her head. Instead of another picture of her family, there was a picture of her on her bed in the black dress I recognized from when I had searched her closet. She looked seductive. Her lips were covered in bright red lipstick and it appeared as though she was kissing the camera.

I looked at the profile a little bit more in-depth and asked Alex, "How does an eighteen-year-old girl with eleven thousand followers drop off the face of the earth and nobody knows about it?"

"A better question to ask is 'What is an eighteen-year-old girl doing on the internet to get herself eleven thousand people to follow her?'" Alex interjected.

"I don't know, but I bet we are about to find out."

I started to shove another piece of pizza in my mouth while I watched as Alex scrolled down the page. What we saw floored both of us. The account was filled with nothing but nude pictures and nude videos of Melanie. Some of the posts even had links to other sites. When we clicked on them, it took us to websites where people could buy videos of Melanie. In them, she was talking dirty, stripping, and masturbating using her fingers and a variety of other objects.

"I can't show these to Chief Cook," I told Alex. "No man should ever see his own daughter doing things like this for money."

"Well, she is really hot," Alex mentioned to me before he pulled his eyes away from the screen. "Although, we shouldn't be surprised by this, Slim. I mean, look at the name she chose for her account." He pointed at the screen where I saw her username: @KissMelDarling.

"Yeah, well too bad she is dead cause now it's more like Kiss Me Deadly or Kill Me Darling."

"Well, now we pretty much know what all the pictures and videos are going to be of. Would you like to take a look at them anyway?" There was a speck of hope in Alex's voice.

"No," I politely told him. "I've seen this girl naked one too many times."

He was confused by what I said.

I didn't want to go into an explanation about how her body was found, so I brought his attention back to the computer screen. "Let's take a look at the account again. It says she has eleven thousand followers, but she's only following one-hundred eighty-seven people. I wonder who those one-hundred eighty-seven people are."

We scrolled through the list of accounts Melanie was following. We discovered almost all of them were either amateur porn stars or amateur porn companies. There was one name among the many I did recognize: Danny Davis.

"Whose Danny Davis?" Alex asked, pulling his horny eyes off the screen for a second.

"He's a strip club owner in Beloit, Wisconsin."

"Wait, didn't you have some trouble with him before you retired?"

I ignored his question and asked him to see if there had been any communication between Davis and Melanie.

He clicked on a tab that allowed the two of us to see all the private messages Melanie had received. There are a lot of creeps out there, and I got a glimpse at just how many wanted an eighteen-year-old girl for their own selfish pleasures. Thankfully, it took Alex less than five seconds to find the conversation I was looking for.

"Jackpot!" I said before reading the business deal the two of them had struck.

Alex observed it too. "It appears their conversation ends after a week of messages and then it probably continued on another account."

"The snake," I growled. "He would do that too."

We went back to the previous page to see if we could find the alias Danny Davis was using. I asked Alex to see if Melanie Cook was friends with Mia Quarry on the Book of Faces or following her on Twitter before we started searching for the alias account Davis was using.

He typed Mia's name into the search bars of both open tabs. "It doesn't look like it. My guess is that Mia has her blocked."

Either that or Mia unfriended her and then blocked her.

I decided to make a phone call to my brother in the hopes of catching him before he went to bed.

"What's up, Josh?" He asked, yawning into the phone.

"Jacob, I need a favor. Know of any way I can get in touch with Mia Quarry?" I asked, wanting to see if I could avoid a full-blown scene with her parents and lawyer present.

"She's serving Mass tomorrow morning at nine."

"Swell. I'll be there tomorrow ten minutes before Mass starts."

He yawned again before asking, "Josh, what's going on?"

I looked at Alex before I continued talking. He was looking through every single one of Melanie's private conversations. I didn't want to explain the whole situation on the phone to my brother, then have to explain it once again to Alex who was sitting right next to me. "I'll tell you later. Right now, I'm in the middle of something, and I need Mia's help with it, but don't want it to turn into a scene. I'll give you more details about what I mean tomorrow."

"Josh, now you've got me worried." I knew he was. He was talking louder than he usually did when he was on the phone.

I had to get him to calm down, or else he'd never get any sleep. "Don't worry. Pray a Rosary or something."

He took a deep breath. "I will do a Holy Hour for you and this case."

"Swell. At the rate I'm going, I hope to have this thing wrapped up in an hour."

My brother's last words that evening to me were, "Be careful, Josh."

I promised him that I would before I hung up the phone and returned my attention to Alex.

It was a good thing I did because Alex had even more bad news for me. "Slim, I gotta tell ya, it seems as though your girl was talking to multiple girls at the same time, all about the same thing."

"What do you mean?"

He pulled up the Facebook account again and showed me messages and comments from a bunch of other girls in Melanie's class. They kept talking about posting pictures, making videos, and meeting up at somewhere they all called 'The Place'.

I had never heard of a place called The Place, but whatever place it was, I had a gut feeling it wasn't a good place to be. Suddenly, remembering the request the chief had given me earlier, an idea came to me. I asked my pal to look at the person who last wrote on Melanie's wall.

He pulled up the post.

I gave him detailed instructions on what to do next. "Now, write a comment on the post saying, 'Sorry I've been sick. I haven't been able to do much or get out of bed, but I'm feeling better now.' Then, I want you to write a new post on Melanie's wall saying, 'I just wanted to let everyone know I'm okay. I am just really sick, and that's all. Thank you for all the love you've been sending me.'"

Once Alex finished typing up the two messages and posting them, he asked me, "What do we do now?"

"We wait," I told him, and a few moments later, a tiny box popped up on the screen. Someone had sent a private message to Melanie.

"Who the fuck is this?" the message read.

I instructed Alex to reply back with, "Melanie, duh."

"Bullshit," the person typed back to us. "I know Melanie, and I know she doesn't type in complete sentences and use punctuation.

"Damn," I thought to myself. I should have told Alex to type like a teenage girl and not use such perfect grammar. I asked Alex if I could take over the keyboard. He let me. It was then that I got a good look at the alias of who was writing to us. At the top of the pop-up box on the screen was a little blue line that had the name Erika Sin on it. To the left of her name was a picture of a skinny teenage girl with a dark tan and jet-black hair wearing a dark-blue tank top that exposed her cleavage. If the name wasn't fake enough, the picture of the skinny girl with the oversized boobs confirmed it.

"Okay, you caught me," I typed back to the phony profile. "Who are you?"

Alex and I finished our crappy beers before the alias responded to us. "I don't have to tell you who I am, Detective Slim."

Both Alex and I were taken aback. Whoever this was, knew who I was, and they possibly knew that I was the one who had Melanie's laptop. I tried to convince them otherwise. "What makes you think I'm Detective Slim?" I typed in the little chat box.

The person typed back, "You can't fool me. I've been watching your every move. In fact, I know you were at the Cook's house earlier this evening."

My mind instantly thought of the man in the black Cadillac SUV. "What do you want?"

The person who was instant-messaging me sent me a request and it wasn't the friendly type. "Look, Slim, all we want for you to do is to just turn a blind eye to our activities, lead the cops in a different direction, and give us enough time to clean up this whole mess with the girl."

"I'm not sure I understand what you're trying to tell me."

Words I didn't believe were appearing before my eyes. "The girl's death wasn't our fault. Accidents happen. All of this is just a big misunderstanding, but it can all be solved in a few days if you just give us the time."

The next words I typed were in all caps. "NO DICE!"

The person I was chatting with gave me an alternative. "Well, if you don't play ball with us, someone else will just have to take it like a champ. Someone like that little Quarry girl."

"You leave her out of this," I shot back before getting irritated and handing the keyboard back to Alex.

"Well, if you want to keep her out of this, you will do your best to keep the police out of this as well," were the demands the person gave us.

"I think it's a little too late for that," I had Alex inform them. "They are already involved, and I'm not going to lie to my boss or my boys."

"Look, we aren't necessarily asking you to lie to them. We are just asking you to take your time in solving this case. After all, you're retired, Slim. We know you have more time than money. We also know you don't have a whole lot to live off of, so let us help you out. You help us out, we'll help you."

Whoever was typing these messages knew more about me than I wanted them to know.

"So, what you're telling me is you want me to buy you some time and in return, you'll buy me a few drinks, and if I don't, you'll find a way to pin this on little Miss Quarry?"

"Exactly," the person typed back before adding a smiley face emoji.

Whoever was typing continued sending me threats. Going on about how Mia was eighteen, and if the court found her guilty, she would be in the clink for twenty-plus years. When she got out of jail, she would be what most women wished they could be: A free woman at the age of forty. A middle-aged woman with nothing holding her back. She would still have plenty of time to get married, have kids, and cross a few other things off her bucket list. Only if she's a good little girl, cooperates, and everything goes her way, knock on wood.

But I knew murder never knocks. It comes in, makes its demands, and if those demands aren't met, it takes what it wants. Much like this person was making of their demands now. So, I had Alex ask them, "What if I don't bite? What if I don't buy any of this? What if I get the Quarry kid out of town before you can get to her? What is your backup plan then?"

"Tell you what," the person messaging me sent before adding more, "I'll give you one hour to type two words to me and those two words are 'I agree'."

"And if I don't?"

The person typing wasn't in the mood for giving me options. "Okay, hotshot, you asked for my Plan B, well, here it is. You might be able to get to the Quarry girl in time, but I know you won't be able to get to Mrs. Cook."

I was getting hot. Now they were threatening Jennifer. Whoever this was, they had already told me they knew I was at the Cook's house this evening. I couldn't let anything bad happen to Jennifer. The man had already lost a daughter; I couldn't let this person take Chief Cook's wife too.

"One-hour, Detective Slim." And then the person I was chatting with sent their last message, "Don't test us."

If there's one thing this job has taught me over the past thirty years, it's that you don't take threats lightly. Whoever this Erika Sin person was, he or she knew all the parties involved in the case, and Erika Sin wasn't afraid to hurt any of them.

"What are we going to do, Slim?" Alex asked me before he stood and allowed his remaining slice of pizza to fall on the floor, so his dog could eat it.

I got off the couch and informed Alex he would stay at home and see if he could find out anything else about the girl who owned this laptop and her pal Erika Sin. Then, I told him he needed to change the password on Melanie's laptop and her social media accounts to my last name, all lower case, so I could easily access everything later. While he was doing that, I would go veer over to the Cook's house and check up on Jennifer.

Chapter 12

The rain beat down so hard on me, it was as if angels were throwing water balloons directly at me. I felt as if time, the city, and the weather were all against me. I must've hit every single red light on East State Street before I finally made it to Perryville. I made the left onto Perryville Street with fifteen minutes left to get to the Cook house before the one-hour Erika Sin gave me was up. I made the right onto Riverside with only five minutes to spare.

I didn't pull into the driveway for fear that whoever was coming after her would see my car and then possibly waited patiently for the opportunity to kill both Jennifer and me. So, instead, I drove my car through the grassy, narrow, and dark back alley behind the houses. I parked my car behind the neighbor's swimming pool. Even if someone looked out the patio door, they would not have been able to see my vehicle thanks to the large deck built around the pool to keep perverts from looking at whoever was swimming. The only way anyone could've possibly spotted my car was if they drove down the same alley I did. I left my car and ran to the front door. I rang the doorbell before pounding my fist on the big green block of wood. My first thought was nobody was home. My second thought was somebody had gotten to Jennifer before I did.

Both of those thoughts were put to rest when Jennifer, still dressed in the outfit she came home from work in, opened the door. "Josh, what's going on? What are you doing here?"

I pushed my way inside the house. "Is Pete here?" I asked while practically hyperventilating. I hadn't run that fast in five years. In fact, I couldn't think of a single reason why I'd ever had to run that fast in the past five years.

"No. He's not." Jennifer said before explaining how her husband left about an hour ago. He told her the guys wanted to get together for late-night practice. Confused by my presence and how I was asking for her husband. She could sense something not good at all was going on.

"Jennifer," I said as I caught my breath, "I hate to break it to you but you are in danger."

"What?" Now she was the one hyperventilating.

"You had a hunch Melanie was in trouble. You had a hunch something bad happened to her. Well, you are right. Now, the men who were after Melanie are after you. Grab your coat. I have to get you somewhere safe."

"Josh, I don't understand." I was confusing her even more.

"Just do as I tell you!" I shouted at her. Like the fool she was, she put on the same shoes she had been wearing all day, the heels that matched her outfit. I ripped her coat from the closet and threw it on her. No sooner did she shut the closet door; did we hear a car door out front slam shut.

"That's them," I whispered in her ear.

"Who is them?"

I put my hand over her mouth. "Never mind, let's go," I said before I pulled her through the kitchen and out the patio doors.

There weren't many places for us to hide outside. So, once we were off the patio, I pushed Jennifer to the ground and rolled her underneath the deck. I followed, squeezing myself under the small space. The ground underneath the deck was mostly dry, but the rain still found a way through the cracks in-between the wood beams. Jennifer tried to talk, but I covered her mouth with my right hand while pulling the gun out of my trench coat with my left. Even though I couldn't shoot worth a darn with my left hand, I had my index finger on the trigger, ready to get a bullet out if I had to.

There were footsteps above us on the deck. We could both hear them. The steps sounded heavy, like a man; a woman would walk more lightly. Whoever it was, they were right above us. All he had to do to find us was walk off the deck, around the side, and if they looked directly underneath, there we would be. But they didn't. Instead, he just walked around the deck, hoping to see if we had taken off through the backyard. Jennifer and I both could see the heels of the man's shoes through the gap between the two pieces of wood that made up the bottom step. I waited to see if the person waiting for us was going to walk through the yard towards the alley. If they did, all he would have to do, is get to the pavement, look left, and they would've seen my car. I held my breath as I held both my gun and Jennifer's mouth.

I thought about crawling out from underneath the deck and shooting the person right in the back but would have had to let go of Jennifer's mouth. Her scream would have given us away in an instant. I stayed where I was. They did the same. Finally, after what felt like ages, the person wearing the black shoes walked back inside the house. I counted a minute down in my head before I put down my gun, took my hat off, and slid the tan object I always carried with me into the grass just to make sure the coast is clear.

When nothing happened to my hat, I slid out from underneath the deck before pulling Jennifer out into the open. She wanted to scream but I grabbed her mouth once more.

"The car is in the alley behind the pool," I whispered in her ear, "Let's go." Instead of running, she turned around and hit me as hard as she could in the arm. She threw another punch and tried to hit me in the chest, but I grabbed her wrist with my right hand. "Do you want to die in your own backyard?" I growled in her ear. "I said, 'Let's go'."

She finally listened, followed me quietly, and got in my car.

I began the drive out of the alleyway. Once I was past the Cook house, I took my time getting out of the alley, driving slowly to avoid all of the potholes.

"Can I scream now?" Jennifer asked sarcastically.

"As long as it's not in my ear, you'll be fine."

She crossed her arms as though she was pouting.

I broke the silence by asking her, "How do I get out of here?"

She was kind enough to give me directions. After I pulled my car onto Riverside, she asked me. "Would you mind telling me, now, what's going on?"

I knew the moment had come where I had to tell her the truth. "Jennifer, you know how you mentioned to me in your kitchen that you thought something awful had happened to Melanie? Well, you were right. Apparently, there was a really bad group of people who were after her. I don't know why or who they are but, I talked to one of them about an hour after I left your place."

She was about to cry, "Dear god, who are they?"

"I don't know."

"Well, if you don't know, how were you able to talk to them."

"I didn't actually talk to them." From there, I explained to her how I'd had a friend of mine hack into Melanie's laptop. We were able to get online, into her socials, and somebody had started chatting with me. Somehow, they knew I wasn't Melanie. Somehow, they knew it was me, and they made a threat. If I didn't call off my investigation or lead the police in a different direction, something bad would happen to her.

"But how do they know where we live?" she asked.

Instead of telling her about the man in the black Cadillac SUV I had seen at the Quarry's, I told her that people have a way of getting all kinds of information over the internet nowadays. Some sites will tell people where you live, where you work, where you shop, and where you go for recreational purposes. There are all kinds of ways to spy on people in today's day and age. I explained all of that to her, and it was in my explanation that I told her someone had known I had been at their house just a few hours prior.

"Well, if they know who you are, and they know who I am and where I live, then we really aren't safe anywhere we go."

She was right. I thought about taking her back to my apartment, but I knew it wasn't an option. "I do know one place where we could go and be safe."

I hopped on Interstate Ninety and took it to Route Twenty. After about twenty minutes of driving, we came to a small town called Winnebago.

I pulled into a wet gravel driveway off a muddy dirt road and parked my car behind the big red barn that was separate from the big red house. I made my vehicle wasn't visible before leading Jennifer to the house.

The color of the siding on the house matched the barn perfectly. The white rocking porch swing complimented both the house and the dark brown porch beneath our feet. The hanging baskets above our heads added the perfect final touch. Although the rain hid the flowers and made the beautiful plants look like white buckets of water with floating flowers in them instead. Still, they gave me a sense of hope that the rest of the night was going to be as peaceful as the floating flowers were. This place brought me both peace and hope, not to mention it had been the best piece of architecture I had seen all day. I wished Jennifer could have seen it in the daytime, especially on a bright sunny day when the property looked like something out of one of those country or cottage magazines.

"The door is locked." She pointed out to me as she drew my attention away from the white hanging baskets.

I jimmied the door open. The moment we were both inside the house, I told Jennifer to take her shoes off, much like her husband had done to me every time I came into their house.

"Is this yours?" she asked, taking off her mud-covered heels and dropping them in the dark.

"No," I told her as I switched on the entryway light. A drinking buddy of mine was out of town until Memorial Day. He had asked me if I could swing by every day and pick up the mail. After remembering that little detail, I ran back outside and got the mail. I threw it in my car, so I wouldn't forget it. When I came back to the house, Jennifer had turned on all the lights in the house. I shouted her name a few times before I heard her voice.

"I'm in the bathroom!" she yelled from behind a closed door upstairs.

I took off my shoes and used the half-bath in the hallway just before the kitchen. Why Jennifer didn't use that one, I do not know. Unless she completely missed it when she was busy turning on every light in my buddy's house. It was a good thing my friend didn't have any neighbors nearby or else the whole situation could have gotten really suspicious really fast.

Once I finished doing my business, I picked Jennifer's dirt-covered navy-blue coat off the floor and walked into the kitchen. I set both of our dirty coats on the chairs.

A voice from upstairs called to me, "Oh, Josh."

I walked to the base of the stairs and looked up to see Jennifer standing above me like an angel. She was even dressed like an angel too. She had traded her soaking wet business clothes in for a solid white bathrobe. She stepped forward as if she wanted to get me to notice the fact that her painted toenails matched her fingernails.

Rather than focusing on her feet, I turned my attention towards the robe she was wearing. "Where did you get that?" I asked.

She shot me a smile before telling me, "I found it in the linen closet. There's one for you too. I thought they would be nice to wear after we took a shower." She untied the robe, letting it slip from her shoulders and waist, and there she stood waiting; the only thing covering her was her bright blonde hair.

I climbed the stairs slowly, not taking my eyes off of her, enjoying every moment of the naked vision in front of me. When I reached the top of the stairs, I kissed her.

She let the robe drop to the floor before she started to take off the necktie I had been wearing for the past two days straight. I helped her with the rest of the clothes I was wearing. We made our way into the bathroom, kissing each other until we got to the tub. I pulled her towards me and held her as tight as I could. She wrapped her right arm around me and used her left hand to turn on the water. I continued to kiss her neck. As soon as the shower was on full blast, we moved under the waterfall together still holding each other. The hot woman in my arms and the hot water running over both of us were the two best parts of my entire day.

Chapter 13

We finished our shower together before we made love on my buddy's bed. Immediately after we finished, she asked me the same question she did when we first got there, "Whose house is this again?"

I reminded her it belonged to one of my drinking buddies, and she asked me what he did for a living.

"You mean what do he and his wife do for a living?"

She gave me a small love tap.

With my eyes toward the ceiling, I told her my drinking buddy and his wife were simple farmers who sold most of their land, then used the money to make some wise investments. They were now spending their retirement living the high life in the tiny town of Winnebago, Illinois.

"Where are they now?" she asked, curious as to what the lovebirds were doing with their second chance at life.

"New Orleans," I told her before explaining they had a daughter down there who was about to graduate from college with a degree she would never use in her life.

She laughed at me before giving me another love tap. We spent the next few minutes cuddling together in silence before she broke it. "I should probably give Pete a call. He might be worried sick about me." She crawled out of bed, and I watched her butt as it moved into the hallway.

I couldn't help but feel as though I had completely ruined the mood. Thoughts of Melanie entered my mind as I'm sure they had her own. Melanie was supposed to graduate from high school next weekend, just like a buddy of mine's grandson was going to.

Jennifer came back into the room holding her cell phone just below her belly button. The light coming from her cell phone gave me a small glimpse of the beautiful naked body I had been cuddling in the dark.

"How's Pete?" I asked before I put my hands behind my head. I'll admit, I did display a bit of cockiness. After all, I was sleeping with the most beautiful woman in town, and he wasn't.

Before the light from her cell phone diminished, I was able to see this look of worry that was on the bottom of her face as she replied, "He said he was still at band practice, which is strange. Normally, they never go this late."

"Did you tell him where you were?"

"Yes, sweetie," she said sarcastically. "I told him I was sleeping with Detective Slim in a beautiful farmhouse on the side of the road."

"You should have given him the address," I said sarcastically back to her. "Then he could have joined us and made it a threesome."

"Ha, you're funny." She laid back down next to me. "I told him I was drunk, and I was spending the night at a friend's house."

"Will he buy it?"

"Oh, he'll buy it alright," she said with confidence. "Pete knows I haven't had a girl's night out in a long time, and he knows when I go out with my friends, I get wasted beyond belief." She slid her hand across my chest and over to my ribcage. "So, what do you do with your retirement besides breaking into people's homes and sleeping with married women?"

"I sit alone in my apartment on Saturday nights and watch those cheesy romantic

Hallmark movies," I told her in the hope she would get a kick out of it.

She played along. "Really? I love the Christmas ones. Which one is your favorite?"

"The one where Santa Claus brings the boy and the girl together, and they fall in love."

"No way! I love that one too."

"Are you being serious? I didn't know there was such a movie."

She laughed before squeezing me as tight as she could. I put my arm around her to cuddle her. We shifted positions to where I was spooning her. She fell asleep. I just laid there staring off into the darkness, wondering if Chief Cook had really been at band practice this whole time or if he was doing something else.

Chapter 14

Despite my comfortable position holding Jennifer, I had a nightmare that night. It was my second one in almost twenty-four hours and it was nearly the same one I'd had the previous night. Only this time, Melanie's dead body came, fully, out of the water. Her dead feet sunk into the live grass as she walked onto the land. Her voice was calm as she spoke to me, unlike last time when she screamed at me as though she were some sort of banshee. "Help me, Josh, help me. Help me before someone else gets blamed."

"Someone else?" I asked the dead teenage girl standing above me.

"Yes, someone else." Her lifeless hand stretched out and pointed to the tree she was found hanging on in the river.

I looked at the tree where she was found. Hanging on the branch that stuck out of the water was Mia. She was tied up much like the way Melanie was when we found her on Friday night. She was still alive and floating in the river. She was fighting with all of her might to catch a breath of air as she bobbed up and down and in and out of the water. Then, the branch broke, and the current pulled her down the river.

I began to run alongside the shore, chasing after her. I saw a large tree stuck in the water, much like the one that caught Melanie's body. I started to climb it. Once I was farther out, I reached down into the water, but Mia went under. I grabbed onto something and pulled it up. As I raised it out of the water, I could tell it was hair but not just any hair. It was human hair. At first, I thought I was pulling Mia up by the hair, but it wasn't Mia. Instead, the hair I pulled up belonged to the decapitated head of a young woman. Her eyes were closed at first, but then they opened, and she spoke to me, "Save them, Josh. There are more lives at stake here than you think."

I woke up in a cold sweat, and Jennifer wasn't next to me. She came back into the bedroom fully dressed and holding my clothes in her arms. "Oh good, you're awake," she said before she threw my suit on the bed. "Get dressed. We have to go."

I rubbed my eyes before asking her, "What time is it?"

"It's six in the morning. I need to be home by seven."

"Why so soon?" I asked, having the idea we could go somewhere in town and have breakfast.

She put that idea to rest when she explained, "Because that's when Pete wakes up."

I put my clothes on as quickly as I could, running down the stairs to use the half-bath one last time before we exited the house.

"Aren't you going to leave a note or something?"

I rolled my eyes at Jennifer. "I have to come back and collect the mail again at some point. I can clean up the house then."

She gave me a smile and blushed a little bit before she brushed her hair gently back with her hand. It was almost as if she was glad someone in her life made her a priority. I was pretty sure her husband rarely ever did that. I watched her walk in front of me. I couldn't help but stare at the mud-covered outfit she had put back on. The only thing missing from it was the black diamond-pattern stockings that she had been wearing the day before. It was nice to see her soft pale legs in the daylight.

The sun had just popped up for the first time in a few days, and it couldn't have picked a better day or moment in time. Jennifer turned around once to face me on her way to the car. The sun fell on top of her, and it was as if I was staring into Heaven itself. She looked at me before looking one last time at the house. "It's such a beautiful place. I wish we could stay here longer."

I looked at the house with her before bringing both her and myself back to reality. "Well, we can't, so let's go."

She didn't say a word to me during the whole drive back to her place. I don't know if it was because she was nervous or ashamed of what we had done last night. Every time I tried to strike up a conversation, she just sat there.

When I pulled up to her house, I asked her one final question. "Are you going to be able to get inside?"

She finally spoke, "Yes, I have the code to the garage door." She had one foot out of the car but pulled it back in before turning around to kiss me. She kissed me twice. The first one was soft and sweet, just like she was. The second one was rough and hard like she wanted to be. "Find my daughter, Josh, find my daughter, please."

I blinked for a moment as I thought about how she repeated herself, much like the way her daughter did in my dreams. I snapped out of it before telling her, "I will. I promise."

She squeezed my hand for a moment before finally getting out of the vehicle.

I watched as those gorgeous naked legs of hers made their way up the driveway.

Before her long skinny fingers pushed the buttons that would allow her back into her own house, she waved her hand sideways as if to tell me to get out of there before her husband saw my car.

I pulled away with my eyes attached to my rearview mirror, watching to see if she got inside. I had nothing to do and nowhere else to go. I didn't want to go back to my apartment for fear of two things. The first reason was that the man in the black Cadillac SUV would be there waiting for me, and the second was that I would fall asleep, missing my chance to talk to Mia. So instead, I pulled into the drive-thru of the first fast-food restaurant I saw, and ordered something quick for breakfast, not forgetting the coffee. I stuffed my face while driving on the way to my brother's church. When I arrived, all those who had attended seven o'clock Mass were making their way to their cars.

I found my brother standing outside, still fully dressed in his vestments, greeting all the people who were leaving. I pulled my car into the lot and waited for him to finish talking to everyone under the sun before I approached him. "Hello, Father," I said, stretching out my hand to greet him as though I were a part of his congregation.

His mouth hit the ground. "Josh, you're a mess. What happened to you? Don't you ever change clothes?"

"Don't you?" I asked as I smiled back at him.

He smirked at me. "The biggest advantage of being a priest is you know what you're going to wear every single day."

"Really? I thought the biggest advantage was being able to make your own work schedule."

"No, that's the advantage of being a private eye. Speaking of which, how is the case going, Josh?"

"I'll tell you about it inside." We went inside and sat down in the front pew. I took a deep breath before telling him, "I spoke to the murderer last night."

"Did you?" He asked, turning his whole body towards me. "Then you know who it is? The case is solved?"

"Not in the slightest. I didn't actually talk to them face to face. We chatted online."

He raised an eyebrow before telling me, "I'm afraid I don't understand."

Like always, I had to spell things out for the person I was talking to, just like I always had to for my brother. "I was able to hack into Melanie's laptop last night and got on her social media accounts. After making a post and telling all of her friends she was all right, her murderer sent an instant message to me under a fake name."

"What was the name?"

"Not that it matters, but I don't think you have an Erika Sin at your school. Do you?"

He rested his head on his hand. "An interesting name, but no."

"That's what I thought. I bet it would be hard for a priest to forget a name like that."

He started to laugh. "It would be hard for anyone to forget a name like that." He turned himself around to face the altar. "What does the killer want you to do?"

"This Erika person wants me to turn a blind eye and lead the police down a different path so he or she or whoever they are can get out of town."

"What happens if you don't do what they ask?"

"The killer will start hurting people. Last night they threatened to kill Chief Cook's wife."

My brother crossed himself.

"She's safe, Jacob. We hid under the deck while the killer was searching their place."

"Well, that explains all the mud on you." He lightly touched my trench coat. "I'm surprised neither one of you got pneumonia." That's my brother for ya, just like my mother, always concerned about other people's health.

"Pneumonia is the least of my worries right now."

"I believe it," he shot back at me before asking, "What happened after the killer left?"

"I took Mrs. Cook somewhere safe."

"What did you do after that?" he asked before quickly saying, "Don't tell me. I don't want to know."

He paused for a moment as if to pray. My brother knew me well, and he also knew how attractive Jennifer was, so it would be no surprise to me if he knew what happened between the two of us.

"So, where does Mia fit into all of this?" he asked me.

I made him aware of the fact that the killer threatened her first.

"I see. So that is why you wanted to know how to get ahold of her." He leaned forward and placed his elbows on the pew as if to think, but he couldn't. Once again, my brother had been stumped by something that didn't have anything to do with theology. With a lack of words of wisdom, he asked me, "In the meantime, what are you going to do before she gets here?"

I leaned back and slid my hands into my trench coat. "Sit here and pray."

"Sounds like a pretty good plan to me," he said before he stood up and started to walk back to the sacristy. "May I ask what you are going to pray for?"

"A solution to this case." I shot him a wink and a smile before returning to my serious tone of voice. "The way things are going right now, finding a solution seems impossible."

Before heading back to the sacristy, my brother gave me a small piece of advice. "If the situation seems impossible, ask for the help and intercession of Saint Rita. She is the patron saint of impossible situations." My brother had a patron saint for everything. I'm pretty sure he could even name the patron saint of douchebags and assholes.

I put the kneeler down using the heel of my right foot. The kneeler made a loud banging sound when it hit the floor. Even as a kid, I loved doing that in churches.

"Josh," my brother said, scolding me, "Be a real private eye for once in your life and try not to draw attention to yourself." What my brother didn't know was, throughout the rest of the day, attention was the one thing I would be trying to avoid.

Chapter 15

I made my way back to the sacristy ten minutes before Mass started. While I was back there waiting for Mia, and staring at the hideous green and tan tile floor that hadn't been replaced in fifty years, my cell phone made a loud buzzing sound. After pulling out the brick I always carried around with me in my pocket, the device told me I had received a text from Sergeant Joey Daniels. The tiny print read, "Troy Dublin arrested for the murder of Melanie Cook. Warrant issued for Mia Quarry."

I sent a message back to Joey asking for information. "Has she been arrested yet?"

My pal sent me a text containing only one word. "No."

I was relieved. I shoved my cell phone back into the pocket of my trench coat just as my client came in through the back door.

"Mia," I called to get her attention.

"Mister Slim?" She wasn't expecting to see me, and I had planned it that way. The distorted look on her face said it all, but the questions coming out of her mouth confirmed it. "What's going on? Why are you here? Why are you covered in mud?"

I ignored all of her questions and got straight to the point, telling her, "Your boyfriend was just arrested for the murder of Melanie Cook."

She changed her facial expression from a distorted one to one that was trying to force a smile. "You're lying."

"I'm not." I gave her the rundown of the situation. "A warrant was issued for Troy's arrest this morning. The police already have him in custody. I just got a text from a friend of mine telling me a warrant has been issued for your arrest as well." I showed her my phone.

My brother walked in and interrupted our private conversation. "Did you tell her about the person trying to murder her?"

"Murder me?!" Mia asked frantically. If she was shocked by what I said, my brother's question put Mia into full-on freak-out mode. "I've just been told I'm about to be arrested, and now, someone wants to kill me as well?!"

"Arrested? What's this about?" my brother asked, giving me a cold stare.

"I hate to break it to you Father, but I just received a text telling me Troy Dublin has been arrested for the murder of Melanie Cook.

The police have a warrant for Mia's arrest as well."

"I can't handle all of this right now!" Mia exclaimed as she threw her hands in the air before stuffing them underneath her armpits.

"If she sets foot on the altar, everyone will see her. I can't have an arrest take place in the middle of Mass," my brother said. Once again, thinking only of himself and the embarrassment an arrest would cause both him and his parish.

"Don't worry. I'm getting her out of here as fast as I can." I tried to grab her arm, but she moved away from me.

"I'm not going anywhere," Mia protested.

My brother stepped out of the sacristy for a moment. Either he left to find himself another altar server or left because he couldn't handle the arguing between Mia and me. When he came back in, there was a look of panic on his face. "Josh, there are a few cops in the back of the church. What are we going to do?"

"What are we going to do? What am I going to do?" Mia asked before she started hyperventilating.

"Calm down," I said before I pulled her into the room where the altar servers changed into their robes. I slid back the doors of a big, wooden closet. After seeing all of the altar server robes hanging there, a lightbulb turned on in my brain. I grabbed Mia by the arm and threw her inside the closet. "Now, stay in here and don't make a sound!"

I shut the doors, but I left it cracked open so she wouldn't hyperventilate more than she already was. I closed the door to the altar server changing room behind me, pulled out my phone, and played with the device as to not look so suspicious.

There was a knock on the sacristy door. Within two seconds of my brother opening it, Chief Cook and four of his men came through it.

"Mister Slim," my employer said to me. I noticed he didn't call me "Detective." He looked around before asking me, "What are you doing here?"

"Just having a small chat with my brother before Mass. Is that okay with you, Pete?"

He gave me that sour grin of his and asked me, "What were you doing last night?"

"Working on the case," I told him before I put my phone back into my pocket. "I was out at the crime scene last night, and as you can see, I fell pretty hard." I opened my coat to show him exactly how much mud I had accumulated.

"I see," he said after he looked me up and down, "well, we have been working on the case too."

"Oh really, have you found anything?"

"Yes, as a matter of fact, I have. We got a hot tip one that of our main suspects was heading here."

"And who might that be?"

"Mia Quarry," he said with pride and without hesitation.

"Interesting," I said before I leaned back and crossed my arms while smearing the dirt from my coat on the walls in my brother's sacristy. I was sure my brother would have someone clean up my mess later.

I ignored what I was doing and asked the chief to tell me more.

My brother interrupted the conversation between the two of us by saying, "Gentlemen, I have to get ready for Mass. You can continue to talk about this subject more back here if you wish, although I would prefer all of you to take this outside. I don't want any interruptions during Mass. Is that understood?"

All of us agreed to the reverend's demands.

After my brother left the room, Chief Cook continued asking me questions. His first one took me aback a little bit, "A little bit touchy, isn't he?"

I shrugged my shoulders before explaining to the Chief how my brother had always been that way, and he just wanted to make sure Mass went off without a hitch. If there is one thing my brother and I had in common, it's the fact that we don't like other people interfering with our jobs.

He made another sour face much like the one he had used on me multiple times while at his house. "Where's Miss Quarry?"

"I haven't the slightest idea," I told him with a straight face.

"You mean to tell me you haven't the slightest idea where your own client is?"

"She's paying me in candy, not cash," I told him before I threw a smile back at him.

"I thought a private eye was supposed to know where his or her client is at all times."

I told him he watched too many movies. He asked me again where Mia was and when I told him I didn't know, he said he didn't believe me.

"Well, you should," I said, removing myself from the sacristy wall and asking him, "Tell me, why are you so interested in finding Mia Quarry?"

He told me about the warrant he had for her arrest before going into the reasons why it was issued. "We have reason to believe both Troy Dublin and she killed my…" he paused for a moment before continuing. Either to compose himself or to not let the officers with him know it was his daughter who had been murdered. He ended his explanation by saying, "…the girl found in the river on Friday."

He lifted his head to look me in the eye, "And I do believe you know where she is."

Shrugging my shoulders and lying to his face, I said, "At home, I guess."

"Wrong!" He yelled directly in my face. He went on to explain how he spoke with Mia's mother before coming to the church. The woman who didn't like me a whole lot told the members of law enforcement that Mia had gotten a ride from a friend to take her to Mass. She was supposed to be serving up on the altar, but she wasn't there.

"I haven't the slightest idea where she is," I said, holding my stance.

The frustration on his face continued to grow until he threatened me. "Slim, so help me, I will take you off this case and rip your paycheck right in front of your face."

I threatened him back. "And I'll bet my paycheck that she isn't anywhere in this church."

He asked his men to leave the sacristy and search the grounds while he stayed back to have a little chat with me. "Look, Slim," he said, putting his hand on my shoulder before he gave me a long-winded speech about how he appreciated me coming out of retirement to help with this case. How he respected my dedication to my client, but the fact of the matter was, I was moving too slow, or at least that was his opinion. Telling me I needed to wrap this thing up, and I needed to wrap it up fast.

Apparently, Jennifer had been asking him questions about Melanie. Probably since our departure from one another, which was still unknown to the chief. He then told me if I didn't solve this case soon, his daughter's picture was going upon the wall of every department store in the area.

I asked him what made him think Troy Dublin and Mia Quarry were behind the death of his daughter, and he gave me an explanation. He had pulled the names of the two people who had found Melanie's body. He asked some of Melanie's friends if they knew who Troy Dublin and Mia Quarry were. They informed him they were classmates of Melanie's, and both of them were bullied several times on several different occasions by his daughter.

He ended his rant by connecting his bloodshot eyes with my droopy ones and saying, "I don't know if you know this, Slim, but in case you haven't read the papers or watched the news stories covering any of the school shootings in recent years. Almost all of them were committed by people who were bullied at one point in time."

I'd had enough of this. Calling me lazy, slow, old, and everything other similar adjective under the sun, I could take. But making assumptions about my client wasn't something I cared to listen to. Even if his assumption was a good one.

I had reached my breaking point and finally just straight up asked, "Are you saying my client is a murderer because she was picked on a few times?"

"I'm saying being bullied is an excellent motive for murder," he came straight out and told me.

This shakedown between us had gone on long enough. Mia was still hiding in the closet behind all of the altar server robes. She was most likely getting claustrophobic and was probably on the verge of passing out, vomiting, or both. I had to change the subject and change it fast. "So, is this what you've been working on all night instead of being at band practice? Hunting down your daughter's friends and asking them questions?"

It worked. I had caught him off guard and was able to change the subject, all at the same time. "Who told you I was at band practice?"

"Your wife did. She told me about it while I dropped her off at a friend's house," I lied.

"Speaking of which, what were you doing with my wife last night Slim?"

I told the truth. "Getting her to safety." Okay, so I told him a half-truth. I went on to tell him most of what had happened the previous night. I told him about how I took Melanie's laptop to Alex and how he'd hacked into it. I also told him we had made a post on Facebook letting people know she was okay, and as soon as we had, someone sent us an instant message. I mentioned they had used an alias to chat with me. Explaining that whoever they were had told me if I didn't steer him and his men in the wrong direction, something terrible would happen to Jennifer.

"Could Mia Quarry have sent the message?" the chief asked me in a non-threatening way. As if he was trying not to accuse my client of, once again, doing something she didn't do.

I had to get his mind off my client. I didn't know how, but then I remembered how the person using the alias threatened Quarry too.

"So, what did you tell my wife when you dropped her off at her gal pal's house?" He asked. Now he was jumping subjects. I don't know if it was because he could tell I was getting overly sensitive about Mia being continuously brought up. Or I was finally doing what I had been trying to do this whole time; get him off the subject of Mia.

Once again, I told him half the truth, "I told Jennifer that something bad had happened to Melanie, and whoever was involved was coming after her next. I told her I had to get her to safety, and she told me to drop her off at her friend's house."

He started to become angry. "And you just left her there?"

"What was I supposed to do? Sit there with a bunch of women and watch her as she's drinking the blues away?"

"No wonder she wasn't home when I stopped by the house. I saw that her car was in the garage, but I had no clue where she went," he said in a peaceful tone before he growled at me again. "Why didn't you call me?"

"Why didn't you call her?" I knew Jennifer's phone didn't go off once the whole time I was with her. I almost gave the chief a chance to know it too, but he was too caught up in the fact that his wife was being threatened by someone who wasn't him.

He paced around the room before telling me, "I thought about calling her, but I was preoccupied with trying to catch Melanie's friends." He apologized to me before saying, "Thank you for getting Jennifer to safety."

I tipped my hat as a way of telling him, "You're welcome."

He composed himself before asking, "So, what just so happens to be the name of the punk who murdered my daughter and threatened my wife?"

I shrugged my shoulders. "Like I told you, he, she, or whoever they are, used an alias. The name that popped up on the screen was Erika Sin."

"It even sounds like an alias."

One of the officers came back into the sacristy. "Chief, we've searched the grounds and the neighborhood. There is no sign of the girl or of the car the girl's mother told us she was riding in."

Chief Cook didn't even look back at the man. He kept his eyes on me and told me, "Look, I'm not going to get into it with you now, but can you meet me at the station in an hour?"

I gave him a wink and a smile and checked my phone. Mia had been in the closet now for close to twenty minutes. "Better make it two. My computer guy is not an early riser by any means. If I show up at his place between now and noon without any warning, he'll think I'm someone trying to rob him."

"Well, tell Snow White to wake up, or else I'll send my seven dwarfs over to his place."

"Fair enough. I'll meet you at the station in two hours." He turned his attention towards the eavesdropper in the room. "Come on," he told the officer standing in the sacristy, "we have to hunt down a missing teenager."

I followed the two men out of the sacristy and sat in one of the pews just in time to hear the end of my brother's homily. I waited for the congregation to stand for The Creed before I went back into the sacristy to check on Mia. I slid open the door and found her curled in a fetal position, clinging onto one of the altar server's robes as if it were a security blanket.

"Is it over?" she asked as she used the robe to wipe the tears off her face.

"If you're asking me if they're gone, then yes. They are gone. If you are asking me if this whole mess is over, not in the slightest."

She stepped out of the closet still holding onto one of the robes.

"You can put that back now," I told her as I softly pulled the robe from her hands. "I believe stealing from a church is a mortal sin."

She let go of it before asking me, "What now?"

"I need to get you somewhere safe where we can talk."

"Okay," she said, still unsure of why she was in so much trouble. We stayed in the sacristy until Mass ended. Then, I followed the crowd outside to make sure the coast was clear. After walking around the church, I opened the back door to the sacristy where Mia had originally entered.

She looked around to make sure the coast was clear before she got into my car. She dove into my backseat and laid down, so no one would see her.

I started to drive and talk, but instead of talking to me, she just played with her phone the whole time. If she didn't want to talk in a moving vehicle, that was fine by me.

Rather than take her back to her parent's house, I took her somewhere close by where I knew she'd be trapped until I got all the information I needed out of her. I took her to the house in Winnebago.

I pulled my car behind the barn like I had the previous night. "We're here," I announced before putting my car in park.

She put her phone back into her pocket, got out of the car, and asked, "What is this place?" She appeared moved by the beautiful scenery around her.

"It's a place where we can talk," I told her before I walked up to the front porch of the house with the red siding. I got inside the house once again without any problem. Once we were inside, I started cleaning up the place.

"Do you live here?" She was puzzled, and I didn't blame her. A bum like me could never own a place like this. Nor did I fit the bill of someone who would live here.

"Nope," I simply told her.

"Then, why are you cleaning up someone else's house?" Mia asked as she watched me run upstairs towards the bedroom Jennifer and I spent the night in.

"Let's just say I had a little bit of fun here last night," I told her without confessing too much.

She laughed. It was probably the first time she'd had a good laugh in two days. She started to climb up the stairs. "Mister Slim, does your brother know you have a naughty side?"

"He's known that since he was three years old when I took his candy bar and blamed it on the dog."

She laughed again, only this time it was harder. It was good to see her laugh.

I finished making the bed, and I told her to get downstairs, so we could talk.

She sat at the kitchen table, but before I sat down, I looked around the floor to make sure none of the dirt that was on Jennifer's clothes or mine had fallen onto the once sparkling tile floor. I wanted to make sure the place was as clean as it was when I had walked in there the night before.

Mia watched me as I looked like an anteater looking for food. "I thought you wanted to talk, not stare at the floor."

She snapped me out of my funk and refocused my attention on her. "You're right, I did want to talk, but I want to make sure nothing was left on the floor from last night."

"You two did it on the kitchen floor last night? Mr. Slim, I'm impressed. Troy and I would never have the guts to…"

"Speaking of Troy," I interrupted her, "let's get back to the reason why Troy was arrested."

She didn't want to talk about it, but she knew she had to. "I take it the police think we murdered Melanie?"

"That seems to be their conclusion," I told her before I pulled up a chair and sat at the table with her. I was now giving her my full attention.

She crossed her arms and her feet and huffed a bit before asking, "What is your conclusion?"

"My job is to protect you and prove your innocence. In order to do that, I need more information."

"I take it the first piece of information you need is to know whether or not I killed Melanie?"

"Unfortunately, yes."

"I didn't. Troy and I found her body floating in the river, and that was it. If I had known I was going to get into this much trouble just for doing the right thing, I would have just let her stay there and float."

I didn't know how to respond, so I threw out a cliché. "It's like the old saying goes, 'No good deed goes unpunished'."

She nodded in agreement before asking, "Is that the reason why they suspect Troy and me? Because we found the body?"

"It's not just because you found Melanie's body," I told her before breaking the hard news to her. "It's also because the police found out you were bullied by Melanie, and for that reason, you are a prime suspect."

"She bullied a lot of people! Why am I being targeted so heavily?"

"Three reasons: One, you found the body. Two, you blocked her on all of your social media accounts. Three, because according to

Jen, I mean Mrs. Cook, Melanie told her she was heading out to see you."

"That lying little puta."

I chuckled a bit before responding to her. "Well, I don't know if she was a liar or a bitch. All I know was that was the last thing she told her mother."

She pouted in the chair for a moment.

"Why did you block Melanie?"

"Why wouldn't I? She was being a bitch to me in real life. Then, whenever I posted something online, she would make fun of me for it the next day."

I changed the subject rather than fight with her about the subject of online bullying. "Does the name Erika Sin mean anything to you?"

She froze. "How do you know that name?"

Finally, I was getting somewhere with this girl. "I was able to hack into Melanie's laptop, and I was able to have an online conversation with this Erika Sin. So, tell me, what's her story?"

"For starters, as far as I know, Erika Sin isn't a she."

"Well, I figured that much. Go on."

"Before I go on, you need to know some things about Melanie." She took a deep breath before giving me a story she had been keeping inside her for a long time about the now-dead girl. Mia told me that when Melanie first came to the school, she had tried to be friends with her.

I could understand why Mia would do such a thing. Coming to a new school in your senior year and trying to make friends is hard enough. Trying to make new friends three months before graduation is even harder.

She continued to tell me a lot of people didn't like Melanie at first. Mostly because everyone knew she was the daughter of the new chief-of-police. But, when people found out she was the oldest girl in the class, and she was already eighteen, a lot of their classmates pressured Melanie into buying cigarettes for them. This worked for a little less than a month before the teachers caught her and someone told her parents. Her folks took away her allowance. Not wanting to lose the so-called friends she already made, she searched for a new way to make money.

"Posting nude pictures of herself online?" I asked.

Mia nodded. "She didn't know where to start, so she opened a new account on a different social media platform. Then started posting pictures of herself with certain hashtags that she figured would draw attention. Then, she said someone sent her a private message and told her if she wanted to make some money, she should do camming, which is filming yourself getting naked online for a live audience."

"Is that where Erika Sin comes into the picture?"

"Sort of," she said, moving her head back and forth before telling me how Melanie started doing camming. The problem was, Melanie could only do it at times when her parents weren't home. So, she came up with a new way to earn money. She uploaded videos of herself to some websites where people could buy the videos and download them for anywhere from ten to twenty bucks, sometimes more. According to Melanie, Erika Sin was one of the people who noticed her. When Sin saw how talented Melanie was with a webcam, Sin asked Melanie to come work for him.

This was where I interrupted Mia's story and asked, "Let me guess, she told the other girls about it too?"

Mia nodded. "You know it. Melanie would brag about it to all of us in the locker room."

"And when the other girls saw the amount of money she was bringing in, they wanted to jump in on the action too?"

"You put two and two together real fast, Mister Slim." She gave me a wink and a smile before becoming serious again and finishing her story. "Melanie started recruiting other girls in the high school once they turned eighteen. They would upload videos of themselves onto thumb drives and sell them to some guy after school."

"I take it this guy was using a fake profile to communicate with the girls?"

"That's what I assumed anyway."

"But why meet with the girls? Why not just have them send the videos to him through the internet?"

"Too risky," she told me, and it made sense. She continued to explain what I had already figured out. If the videos were going to a specific website or e-mail address, the FBI could track them. Plus, by giving the video files directly to somebody on a flash drive, the girls could get paid cash on the spot and the buyer could get a good look at the girls he was getting videos from. This way, he could see what he was buying, in a sense, and he could recruit the prettier girls for other things.

This is where my curiosity peaked, and I asked Mia, "What other things?"

She didn't say, but it didn't matter.

I had the information I needed, so I told her, "Come on, let's get you home."

"Ah, Mister Slim," she said, staring at her phone. "I don't think home is the best place to take me. My mom has been blowing up my phone asking me where I am. Apparently, the cops left the church and went back to my house, and some of them are still waiting."

"Fine by me," I told her before standing up to inspect the kitchen one last time. "I'll take you somewhere else."

Chapter 16

I had fifteen minutes to get to Alex's house, pick up the laptop, and get to the police station. On top of it all, I had to find a place to hide Mia.

"Where are we going?" she asked me.

"To a friend's house," I told her.

After pulling into Alex's driveway, I escorted Mia to the door. The neighborhood's ruffians were hooting, hollering, and doing everything they could in their possible power to get Mia's attention.

I rang the doorbell twice before Alex opened the door and asked, "Who is she, and what is she doing here?"

I grabbed Mia by the arm and walked inside the house with her. "Her name is Mia, and she is wanted by the police," I told him before I shut the door behind us. "I need you to hide her here while I deal with the police and explain to them everything we found out last night."

"You can't hide her here," he protested. "She's a teenage girl. There's nothing here for her to do or eat."

"Well, show her what you do for a living. Talk to her."

"I can't talk to women," he said before giving me an explanation that didn't hold water. "I'm a thirty-year-old bachelor. If I start talking to her about computers and web design, she'll become bored within fifteen seconds. Just like every other woman I talk to about the subject."

"Take her golfing!" I screamed at him. "It's the first sunny day in a while. You, yourself, could use some sun. You've probably been wearing the same clothes for days now."

"So have you!" He noticed I was wearing the same suit I was wearing yesterday.

I looked around his house, found the laptop, and took it. "Did you do what I asked?"

"Yeah, but..."

"Good! Now, I have to be at the police station in six minutes. Get dressed, take her golfing, and text me when you get to the course. I will meet you two there as soon as I'm done at the police station."

I left the house with the laptop in my hand, leaving Mia standing in Alex's mess of a living room with wide eyes. As I was walking to my car, one of the local ruffians shouted to me, "Hey, where's your girl?"

"In the living room, cleaning her gun," I told him before getting in my car and leaving.

I arrived at the police station with two minutes to spare. Granted, I had been going sixty-five in thirty, but no one honked their horn or got in my way.

I walked into the police station with less than a minute to spare. Chief Cook was standing by the doors waiting for me.

"Right on time," he said. "I thought you'd be early."

"I may be retired, but I've got things to do."

"I see," he said as he looked down at the laptop I was carrying in my hand. "Come on, let's go to my office."

We walked into his office, and before we got down to business, we closed the door and the blinds.

"Alright, let's take a look at everything you've found," he said to me before he took a seat in his chair.

I turned it on in front of him. When a bar on the screen popped up asking me for a password, I typed in my last name all lowercase. Alex had done as I had asked, and I got in without any problem. The thirty-year-old hobo had done well.

Chief Cook glared at the screen. "What are we looking at?"

"Your daughter's life outside of school," I told him as if he was stupid. In a big way, I still thought he was. I pulled up one of the videos Melanie had taken of herself.

It made him sick to his stomach.

"That's just the tip of the iceberg," I told him before I clicked the icon to head to her Facebook page and pull up the conversation between Erika Sin and me.

I had him read the whole thing between the two of us. Then I had him scroll up to see the previous conversations that his daughter had with this particular individual.

It infuriated him. "Do we know what the name of 'The Place' is?"

"I still haven't figured that one out," I told him before I stepped away from the desk.

Allowing him to see more of the distasteful material on his own, "But, I do have a clue." I came back to the laptop and pulled up another one of Melanie's social media accounts. I showed him the account of one of the people his daughter was following. It just so happened the person to who the account belonged was following her back. "Do you recognize that name?" I asked, pointing at the screen.

He left his chair and walked over to the window where a box of tissues was collecting dust. He pulled a few of the bright white snot collectors out and wiped his face with them. He spoke with the open air for a moment, "Oh Melanie, Melanie, Melanie, of all the people you had to be involved with, why did it have to be him?"

"Sir?" I called him out of respect, given the sensitivity of the situation.

He turned around and addressed me, "Slim, please have a seat."

We both sat down in our respective chairs: He at the big black one behind his desk and me at the one in front of his desk with the wooden armrest and the soft red padding. He started the conversation by asking me, "How well do you remember Chief Rawson?"

I thought a moment to recollect the memories I had of my old boss. I watched my words. "He was a good man. He did everything by the book. He…"

"He hated you," Cook interrupted me.

"Well, nobody likes to say anything bad about anybody after they've died."

"Rawson thought you were unorthodox." He didn't have to say more than that, but he did. Everything that came out of his mouth was everything I already knew. Rawson thought I cut corners and then some. He thought I was unruly, undisciplined and didn't like the fact I used my own methods to get the job done. When he looked at me, he saw a vigilante but had always said that I got the job done. Cook must have known all of this because Rawson was my partner before he took the job as Chief of Police here in Rockford. He had also been a role model and friend to the now Chief Cook.

"Wow, it really is a small world after all," I said to him, "But what does this have to do with the case?"

He continued. "After you retired, Rawson pulled the unsolved case you had been working on. He started to work on it himself. He would call me up and tell me about it. 'If only I could solve this one case,' he would say to me, 'I could die telling everyone, I beat Josh Slim.'"

He let out a heavy sigh before he continued on with his small speech. "The night Melanie died, and you were standing here in this office, I was hesitant to hire you. Then I thought to myself, 'If I could solve the case of my daughter's death before this guy can, then I could fulfill my friend's last dying wish.' His last wish was to show you up and to prove to everyone in this precinct that Josh Slim isn't all he's cracked up to be."

"Flattery will get you nowhere, sir," I told him, while I was watching him reach down in one of the drawers in his desk for something I couldn't see. I had my right hand in my trench coat and my finger on the trigger of the antique .45 I was carrying around with me.

Instead of pulling a gun, he pulled out a large file. "Here," he said before throwing it at me. "This is everything we've got on Danny Davis."

I thumbed through it a bit. "This is quite a lot. It looks like it's eighty percent of my stuff, fifteen percent of Rawson's stuff, and five percent of your stuff."

"Thank you for giving credit where credit is due," he said sarcastically before getting serious again. "You need to look at the file more closely. You won't believe your eyes."

"Sir, as much as I enjoy reading. I was wondering if you would mind just giving me the cliff notes version of everything both you and Rawson found out after my departure."

"If you want it that way, to sum it up in one short sentence, Davis has gone viral."

"Okay, that was short. Do you mind giving me a little bit more detail?"

He filled me in on the things I had been missing since my retirement. "After the run-in the two of you had, he figured out that strip clubs no longer brought in the money or the clientele they used to. Let's face it. Strip clubs originally started out as gentlemen's clubs where men in overpriced suits paid for overpriced drinks and to have overpriced girls dance on their laps. Now, they are old broken-down buildings, with old broken-down men who drink beer from a can and give their last five bucks just to get a tease out of a small-town single mother."

He continued this history lesson for a few more minutes before telling me how the internet changed everything. Now a guy can sit in the privacy of his own home, where nobody judges him, and view all the girls he wants, all for one low monthly fee.

It was here that I had a chance to stop him in the middle of his story, and I took it. "So, what you're saying is, Davis keeps the strip club open, but he's running porn sites on the side?"

"Precisely." He stood up, put his hands in his pockets, and started to walk in circles around his office.

I just sat in my chair with both my hands in the pockets of my trench coat, waiting for him to drop a bomb.

And he did. "What Davis is doing with the sites is just one part of his master business plan. Rawson and I believed he would get these girls to make videos of themselves, and he would pay for them with cash, then post them on his website. After that step was done, he offered them even more money by recruiting them to come and work for him at his strip club. Rawson and I believed that was part two. Once the girls put their complete trust in him, he would move to step three and sell the girls as sex slaves."

I was confused for a second. "You mean to tell me Davis is running a human trafficking operation out of Naughty-or-Nice?"

"We have every reason to believe so." He shook his head before he continued to pace around the room. "We believe he is recruiting girls from Illinois, bringing them across the state line, and selling them in Wisconsin."

I knew Davis was a monster, but I didn't think he was this big of one. "I hate to admit it, but it sounds like a good plan. Illinois girls go missing; Wisconsin authorities don't have to deal with it."

"It was a good plan," Chief Cook admitted, "until my daughter got involved. He pulled a gun out from the top drawer of his desk.

"Wait a minute," I told him as I sprung up out of the chair. "You can't honestly tell me you plan on going after Davis by yourself?"

"Why not?"

It was obvious I had to explain to him the severity of the situation. I told him about how Davis has been doing this kind of work since the early nineties. How he's no fool and he knew his clientele well. I told him I was trying not to be judgmental but, from my personal experience, I knew only four types of men go to strip clubs: Men with money, men with attitude problems, men with drugs, and men with badges; and Davis knew how to deal with all four.

"Well, he hasn't dealt with me!" Chief Cook said with a boldness that was ready to take on the world.

I grabbed his bicep and gave it a hard squeeze. "If you go in there by yourself, you'll be killed. Davis himself may never carry a gun, but he has at least four men around him at all times who do."

He pulled himself away from me. "Then I'll get a group of men, and we'll go after him together."

"Wait a minute," I protested, grabbing him by the collar and pulling him back to reality. "You can't go all cowboy, riding into Naughty-Or-Nice with men and guns without a search warrant."

"Why the hell can't I?" Chief Cook said, pulling out of my grasp.

I tried to talk some sense into him. "Think about everything Rawson taught you. Think about doing things by the book."

"Fuck the book," he said. "That worm killed my daughter."

I grabbed him by collar again and screamed at him, "You don't know that for sure!"

What was I saying? I had been chasing after Davis all the way up until the day I retired. I should have been encouraging this man to go after the sicko with every available resource he had. Instead, I was holding him back. Why? What had changed inside of me? Six months ago, I would've pumped Davis with enough bullets to make him look like a piece of Swiss cheese. Now, I wanted to see him rot in jail. It was as if I thought God should end the fight between the two of us His way and for us to see who would die first of natural causes.

Chief Cook began tearing up in front of me. "You're right," he said, taking a sleeve and brushing it across both his eyes. His eyes were red, first with sorrow before they were filled again with rage. "But he might as well have. He took my baby girl away from me and turned her into one of his little sex objects to dangle in front of other perverts like him. All so he could make a quick buck."

"That's true, but you're not the only parent whose life has been affected by Davis's actions."

"You're right," he said, wiping his eyes one last time with his sleeve again and pulling himself away from my grip. He walked over to his desk, picked up the laptop, held it in the air, and waved it like a baby's rattle. "I have everything I need right here." Then he came over to me and shook the small computer in my face. "All the conversations Melanie had with Davis himself and her girlfriends. The moment I show this to the parents of these girls, they will lose their shit. Parents of this town will be fully behind me and support me for taking down Davis the way I plan to. If Judge Billsland and Mayor Halstead want to be re-elected, then those two ladies will see my actions as just."

"And Rawson called me a vigilante," I said with disgust to the man who replaced my former boss. "If Rawson were alive and here right now, he would tell you that you have made this too personal, and you should back off and let him take it from here."

"Davis made it personal first!" The chief made a point of making sure I knew it. "My daughter is dead, and I'm not going to let some sex maniac ruin other people's lives as well."

He slid open another drawer, grabbed a notepad and pen, and wrote a message on it. When he was done, he handed the note to me and said, "Here you go, Detective Slim. Congratulations, you solved the case before Tuesday morning. You can take that note to the clerk's office anytime you want to, and she'll cut you a check."

I looked at the note. Chief of Police Cook was giving me twice as much as I expected. "What about the Quarry girl?" I asked, trying to distract him from his rage.

"What about her? Troy Dublin was released earlier this afternoon. His parents and their attorney came down to get him. The kid was crying the entire time he was here. I couldn't hold him. Now, I have no reason to go after him or little Miss Quarry. We know who my daughter's killer is. Now if you'll excuse me, Detective Slim, I have to make a few phone calls." He sat down at his desk and started pushing buttons.

I looked at my phone. Alex had sent me a text message. All it said was, "I took the girl golfing like you told me to. She took off running the moment we got there. She said she had to go. She said she saw her family's lawyer at the golf course and was heading to a friend's house nearby. I tried to stop her, but I couldn't."

"Just my luck," I thought to myself. I put my phone back in my pocket before I walked out of the office. I wasn't sure what was going to happen to Mia. I wasn't sure what was going to happen to Chief Cook. I wasn't sure what was going to happen to Davis. I was only sure of one thing. I was sure that I had to make it to Naughty-or-Nice before Chief Cook did.

Chapter 17

Believe it or not, just over the Illinois/Wisconsin border, there wasn't always a hot spot to see hotties. In fact, Naughty-or-Nice was once a Christmas store. It was called Christmas Land, and its main room once held over a thousand different Christmas decorations. It had six side rooms, all of which were different themes: one room was for moving figurines, another was for lights, another was for wrapping paper, another was for Christmas cards, another was for Christmas music and movies, and I could swear the final one was just for tinsel. I remembered going there with my brother whenever he came home from the seminary. Once the big-box department stores started moving into the area and selling Christmas merchandise cheaper than the cozy little mom-and-pop store, the store closed its doors.

Davis, who had recently closed down one of his other strip clubs off the Illinois Tollway during that time, saw an opportunity in the once fun family-owned facility that sat on the entrance into Wisconsin. Keeping with the Christmas theme, he named the place Naughty-or-Nice, and boy was it a hit.

The candy-cane-painted pole that held the new neon sign must have stretched over fifty feet in the air. The red and green lights could be seen all the way from the highway. The bright neon sign on top of the candy cane pole featured not only the club's name but also a neon outline of a girl in a skimpy Santa suit kicking her leg up and down. The green building with its red roof and white gutters added even more to its Christmas theme.

I pulled into the parking lot, got out of my car, and looked up at the sign. Underneath the candy cane striper kicking up and down was a sign that Davis had recently added that said, "Open all year round".

"Yeah, I bet you are," I whispered to the wind before walking inside the club. I was stopped by a big guy who wasn't wearing an elf costume but instead was dressed in a black tuxedo with a red bowtie.

He wasn't very merry when he told me, "Twenty bucks to get in here, pal."

I pulled out a different bill. "I'll give you the whole hundred if you tell me where Davis is."

"That won't be necessary, Detective," a man said from behind me. It was the same man I had seen driving the black Cadillac SUV. "Detective Slim, follow me." The man led me inside and to one of the old side rooms. If I remembered correctly, it was the one that used to have the moving figurines of Santa, snowmen, reindeer, and other things your neighbors would like to steal from your yard.

The man searched me, found the antique .45, and took it for himself. I didn't move, but I soon found myself planted into an uncomfortable brown wooden chair. In front of me was a hardwood desk, and behind that desk was Davis. He had put on a few pounds since the last time I saw him. Either that or the red camel-haired sport coat he was wearing just made him look bigger than he really was. The black button-down dress shirt and the solid red necktie he was wearing complimented the jacket well.

"Nice outfit," I told him before adding, "but don't you think you're really going a bit overboard with this whole Christmas theme? I mean, after all, it is May, you know."

He sat there and ho, ho, hoed at me a bit. "I'm Santa Claus all year round."

"Yeah, I bet you are. A Santa Claus who supplies people with real-life sex dolls."

"Come now, Slim," he broke character, "do you really think a guy like me would be involved in something as dirty as human trafficking?"

"You've never been afraid of getting your hands dirty in the past."

The goon who took the .45 from me handed it to Davis. "And I see you aren't afraid of getting your hands dirty in the present." He put the gun in the pocket of his suit coat before getting out from behind his desk. "Look, Slim, this business is as clean as any business can be, or should I say as clean as a strip club can be. But you are not here because of my club. No, I know why you are here, Slim. You are here because of the videos I have been buying from the legally aged high school girls. Well, all I have to say about the subject is, I am doing nothing illegal. All I am doing is purchasing the videos they take of themselves and redistributing them for a profit. Everything I am doing is perfectly in line with free-market capitalism."

After listening to his speech, I made him listen to mine. "And if the girls get enough views, you recruit them to come and work for you. Is this your latest business plan? You send your group of 'girl hunters' from here out to high-school campuses. You pay those innocent young girls to take pictures and make videos of themselves. Then, you post them on your websites, see how many views they get, and if your audience likes them, you hire the girls to work in your club?"

"I am merely giving them a job opportunity." That was the way he saw it. Davis asked me if I truly felt that these kids nowadays wanted to work in fast-food or in retail?

He was right in that sense. After all, we were now dealing with "The Entitlement Generation". Kids who don't want to work hard, and it's true. You can drive up and down any busy street in America and see a now hiring sign every two blocks you go. Every business out there is recruiting. Why should strip clubs be any different? These kids nowadays grew up being told they were special. Then, they get out in the workforce, discover they are not special, and that they're just bottom feeders. But they don't want to be bottom feeders. No! They want to be stars and just be handed the opportunity to be stars. Davis fulfilled that fantasy by giving them the false impression they could be.

It was all a lie, and I let him know it. "From stars to strippers to slaves. You remind me of that guy in Pinocchio who brought all the kids to Pleasure Island and then turned them into donkeys."

He slammed his fist on his own desk. I didn't know if he did so because he was frustrated that I was right or because I had just compared him to a fat, old man in a Disney cartoon. "I've had enough of you, Slim!"

"So have most people. But you have to admit, a lot of people have had enough of you too. In fact, I don't know a jury in either Illinois or Wisconsin that would convict me for killing you."

He laughed at my comment. "And why do you say that?"

"All my lawyer has to do is tell them I killed the man who had killed Melanie Cook. And that the same man had also posted a bunch of nude photos and videos of barely legal teenage girls online."

He sat back down in his chair. "You want the truth about the Cook girl? Fine, I'll tell you the truth. I found her online. She was using some of my favorite hashtags I use to promote my own business. So, I decided to follow her. I liked what I saw, and so I sent her a direct message. We chatted privately for a bit. She told me she was eighteen years of age and gave me the name of the high school she went to. Then, I sent Dustin over there to check out her story. She was real, and so were her friends. They had a product we wanted. We bought it, repackaged it, and resold it in the true American way."

He took a deep breath, brushed his tongue against his lips, and continued. "On the night she was supposed to come here and work, I thought she had chickened out. I sent her a text message, but I didn't hear back from her. I came to find out later that her body was discovered in the river. She was murdered. I sent Dustin to the home of one of my other girls to see if it was all true. The only problem was, you got there first."

A door opened, and Mia walked into the room. She was dressed in a white bikini top with a short white skirt with thin pieces of cloth coming from it that made it look like a hula skirt. She stood there with her head bowed, looking down at the floor. She said nothing. All she did was stand there and breathe through her nose.

Davis continued to talk and talk he did. "You see, Slim, ever since you showed up at my door a little over a year ago, I have trained all of my men to recognize both your face and your vehicle. Dustin was waiting outside the Quarry house to talk to Mia that day because she had texted me and told me all about the dead body she and her boyfriend had found in the river. When you got back to the vehicle, Dustin had me on speakerphone, and I sat in this chair and listened to him tell me every detail about the man who walked out of the house. When I knew it was you, I began to prepare my men for your arrival. I even had Dustin follow you for a while until I needed him back here at the club to conduct real business. Believe it or not, even bouncers call in sick sometimes."

"I would call in sick every day if I had a boss like you. You disgust me," I spat at him, but my phlegm didn't go very far. Then, I looked at Mia and added, "The both of you do."

"Oh, come now, Slim, what I am running here is a legitimate business. What she is doing is merely working for me. We are not monsters, nor are we conspiring against you. We are simply employer and employee. In fact, Mia is no more Melanie's killer than I am."

"So, who killed her?"

"I'm afraid I don't know the answer to your question. Nor do I care to know. It's out of my hands."

"So, what you're telling me is you view yourself as being no different from any other employer out there. Nobody is special. Everyone is just an able body their boss can dispose of at any moment in time?"

"Why, Slim, you make manual labor sound so cruel. It's not like that at all. Physically, yes. I have lost Melanie as an employee, but," he stopped his rambling for a moment to pull out his cell phone, "through technology, she will live forever."

He went on to tell me his plan. He intended to upload the videos he had of her on a thousand different sites. Now, he could continue to make money off her without having to cut her a paycheck or print her out a W-2 at the end of the year.

"Her image will be with us forever, but her physical presence, well, you lose one girl, you find another, that's business, that's life." That was his explanation.

After he finished with it, I decided to open up old wounds. "Is that what you told that one girl before you had your men chop off her head?"

He started to laugh as though I had made some sort of joke. "Still hanging onto that, are you? How long has it been, Slim? Over half a year ago? When will you learn to put the past behind you?"

He turned his attention towards Mia. "My dear, you told me a lot of things in the past hour. You've told me a lot about Slim, but there is one thing he didn't tell you about himself. That one thing is, he is absolutely crazy. He's completely paranoid. He thinks just because a girl's body was found near this establishment, I had something to do with it. He said many things to you, dear. Now, there is one thing I am saying to you." He took a small break from speaking, and taking his index finger, he put it under Mia's chin and used it to lift up her head. They gazed into each other's eyes for a second before he uttered two words to her, "You're fired!" Then he ordered one of his goons to go in the back and get Mia's things.

"Are you happy now, Slim? Are you happy someone gets to walk out of here alive and unharmed? Are you happy I let her go back to her normal life? Are you happy I just lost someone who could have been one of my best girls for the next ten years?"

"You lose one girl; you find another. That's business. That's life," I said, throwing his own words right back at him.

One of Davis's goons came back into the room through the door behind us. He handed Mia a large purse containing her stuff. She was still standing with her head down like she had been when she came into the room. She held onto her things the same way she had in the robe closet when I had gotten her after Chief Cook and his goons left the church.

Davis looked at both of us before he crossed his arms. "Now leave, or do I need my boys here to show you both the door?"

I got out of the chair and walked over to Mia. I grabbed her by the arm and said, "Let's go."

She pulled away from me and walked out of the room first.

I followed the glitter-covered white strings coming off of her skirt right out the door. I called out her name a few times once we were both outside the club. "Mia, Mia!"

She didn't answer. She just kept walking.

Finally, I told her, "This is not the type of life you deserve."

"How do you know what I deserve, Mister Slim? I mean, who are you to judge me?" She had a point. She went on to tell me that in one week, she was going to graduate high school with a D average. No college would accept her, and it's not like she'd be able to afford one anyway.

After telling me about her academic situation, she told me about her personal one. "I may be an only child, but neither of my parents have glamorous jobs. My mom has been carrying the family financially for the past year. My dad has changed jobs three times in the past two years. If I am ever going to make a decent living and fulfill my dream of getting my own car and moving out of that house. I'm going to have to use every resource I have available to me, and right now, the best resource I have is my own body."

"What would your grandfather think about what you've been doing, or what you just said?" I let it soak in for a moment.

It started to rain.

She started to cry.

I took my trench coat off and wrapped it around her. I picked her up: One arm under her knees and the other around her shoulders. Carrying her over to my car, I said, "Come on, kid. I'll take you home."

I opened the passenger side door of my car and slid her inside. I never realized how much mud made its way onto high-heeled platform shoes until she slid them off her feet. The white strap of the shoe that wrapped around the back of her heel left a big red mark. If walking in those things was bad enough, I couldn't imagine dancing in them."

I went around to the driver's seat and got inside.

"I take it we're heading back to my parent's house?"

"Yep," I told her.

"I take it you are going to tell them everything that happened?"

"Nope," I told her.

"Why not?"

I locked eyes with her, "Because you are going to tell them everything that happened, but first, you are going to tell me everything that happened. My first question is this, was the story you told me the truth, or was it just bull?"

"It was one-hundred percent true."

"Well, then, why did you get wrapped up in all this?"

"I wanted to be popular!" she screamed at me. "I wanted to be like all the other girls." She began to weep uncontrollably in my car.

I put my arm around her and used my good cop voice. "Hey, kid, there's nothing wrong with wanting to be liked. In fact, it's a natural human thing. We all want to be liked by everyone we meet. We all want people to accept us for who we are." I took my arm off of her. "Now, tell me, how did you get wrapped up in all of this?"

She gave me the truth as she remembered it. She had heard stories in the girl's locker room after gym class. They would talk about the videos they made and how much money they sold them for to the man in the black car. One day, she skipped her last class, and she met the man in the parking lot. Mia asked him if she could make money too. He only asked her two questions. Was she eighteen, and did she have a wire on her? She answered both questions with a firm "No".

The man in the car had smiled in reply before telling her he could make her a star. He asked her to take some pictures and make a few videos of herself like the other girls had. She decided to haggle with him. Telling him the money he was paying the girls for their flash drives wasn't enough. Mia told him she wanted the big money. He smiled at her and, according to her, said, "Well, kid, if you want the big money, you have to audition for the boss." That was when he gave her Davis's business card. She got an audition, then she got a job working weekends at the strip club, and that's how she got involved.

"So, you didn't drag Melanie Cook into this?" I asked.

She was offended I would ask such a thing. "No, Mister Slim. I swear I didn't."

I believed her. I believed her like any grandfather would his own granddaughter, no matter what story she told him.

"Will you answer me one question?" She brushed her hair back as if she was no longer ashamed to show me her face. "Why do you and Mister Davis hate each other so much?"

I took a heavy sigh before I told her the truth that I wanted everyone to forget. I told her how Davis had been the primary suspect in my last case with the police department. I was personally asked by the Beloit Police Department to help them with a murder case they were working on. A girl was found dead in the dumpster at the edge of the parking lot of Naughty-Or-Nice. Someone had chopped her head off and threw her remains in the dumpster. Davis only had trash pickup once a month, and the body had been sitting in there for a while.

She took a hard swallow before asking me, "How was it discovered?"

"One of the garbage men found it. He was looking into the rearview mirror as the dumpster was being emptied. He told the police for a moment there, he thought women were falling from the sky."

She giggled. Then she apologized for doing so. At least she wasn't crying anymore. "What happened next?"

I finished my story by telling her that Davis had been brought in for questioning. He'd said he had no clue who the girl was. He kept telling us someone else had thrown the body in the dumpster. He kept telling us someone was trying to frame him. The girl had no identification on her. We couldn't identify her by her dental records or her fingerprints. We even tried to identify her by her facial features. That didn't work either. Then again, when you've had a months' worth of trash piled on top of your head, your face would be a mess too.

"No one came forward saying that one of their loved ones was missing?"

"Nope," I said, taking a deep breath and doing a small wiggle in my seat. Continuing on, I told her how we had even brought all of the employees at the club in for questioning. None of them had ever seen her before. We even told reporters what she was wearing when the garbage men found her. She'd had on a thin, backless, purple shirt and a pair of black dress slacks at the time of her death. Those were the only two pieces of clothing she had on her. We didn't even find her shoes. In the thirty years that I had been on the force, she was my one and only Jane Doe.

"What makes you think Davis was lying about not knowing who she was?"

She was asking a lot of questions but answering all of them was becoming almost therapeutic for me. I began to explain my reasoning to her. For starters, the estimated time of death was around five-thirty in the morning, which is the same time his establishment closes. Davis said he was already in bed by then. However, one of his neighbors, who leaves for work around the same time Davis normally gets home, said Davis got home that day at his usual time.

The second thing was the inconsistency of the girls' testimonies. We should have brought all the girls in at once, but we hadn't.

The first group of girls answered the questions we presented to them one way. Then the second group came in answered the questions differently. Afterward, girls from both groups kept coming back to the station, wanting to change their stories.

The third and final thing that made it seem Davis was lying was what we found out from three of the girls working there. Some nights there would be occasions where new girls would show up at the club. They weren't regular employees at all, but rather, they were brought in specifically for VIP customers.

"And that was when you thought Davis was involved in human trafficking?" she asked in a low, shy voice.

I acknowledged her deduction but told her the problem was I still couldn't prove it.

"So, you planted evidence?"

"No," I said before confessing, "I hid a microphone in Davis's club instead. Without any authorization to do so."

"What happened?"

"He found it, and he told my boss." I let her figure out the rest on her own.

My boss was irate. He ripped into me not only for spying but also for getting too involved in another police department's business. Two days after being chewed out, I announced my retirement. My boss never apologized to me, and I never apologized to him. He died of cancer a few weeks before Peter Cook took over the department.

"I'm sorry," she said, grabbing my bicep the same way I had grabbed hers before she stormed out of the club.

"The only thing you have to be sorry for is for getting up on that stage and showing off your goods to men who are two-to-ten times your age."

She smiled. I took it as I sign that the message had gotten across to her. "Well, it was fun while it lasted."

It made sense to me why she had done it, and why it had been appealing. A child not appreciated by her father steps up onto a stage where she is worshiped and adored by men her father's age. An unpopular kid at school gains the attention of a room full of people the minute she starts taking off her clothes. An outcast by her peers finds support in a group of women who are in the same financial situation she is in, if not worse.

I had one final question for Mia. "What does Troy think about all this?"

"He doesn't know," she said, sitting back in her seat and staring out the windshield, watching the rain. "I tried to keep him in the dark about all of this by telling him I was working weekends at the airport."

I wondered for a moment exactly how many people she had been lying to since she started this job. I started the car, and we started moving. We started talking about happier things, and the small talk continued once we were on the highway. Then, something caught my eye. Before I made the turn to get onto I-39 South from I-90, I saw six police vehicles. All of them were in the same lane, and all of them were following behind one another.

"Hold on," I instructed Mia. I got onto I-39 South, got off at the first exit, made a u-turn, and got back right on the highway.

"What's going on?" Mia asked as we headed in the direction we had previously come from.

"There is going to be a raid," I explained to her. "Chief Cook and his men are going straight to Naughty-or-Nice, and they are going to get Davis".

"Can they do that?"

"Unless Judge Billsland issued a warrant, they aren't supposed to, but it doesn't matter to Chief Cook. I told him this afternoon how Melanie had been making videos of herself and selling them to Davis. He is convinced Davis murdered his daughter."

"What drew him to that conclusion?"

"I don't know," I said sarcastically, "maybe it's because the man's business was being watched by the police for almost a year. Then the moment the police turn their heads, the guy starts buying pornographic videos from eighteen-year-olds. Some of the videos just so happen to have the daughter of the chief of police in them." I could tell I was making her feel dumb. I was about to make her feel even dumber. "You didn't, by chance, tell Davis about Melanie Cook being the daughter of the chief of police, did you?"

She let her head shrink into her shoulders as if she were a turtle. "I might've let it slip out once or twice, but I think he already knew."

I shook my head.

"Look out!" she screamed at me before bracing herself.

I swerved to miss the car I had almost slammed into. "Between my physical presence and your loud mouth, Davis is probably prepared for this." I tried my hardest to catch up to the squad cars, but it was no use. There were too many semi-trucks merging onto the highway at the same time. When I tried to get around them, there were just too many other cars moving out of their way like I was. I screamed multiple profanities in the car.

"Ouch, my virgin ears," Mia said sarcastically. The kid was getting the hang of my humor.

"Yeah, well, dressed in that getup, you look like anything but."

As soon as we crossed back across the state line, the weather got worse. The rain was so heavy, it was as if water balloons were falling from the sky.

"Can't you go any faster?" Mia asked me in typical teenager fashion.

"I would be able to if I could see better."

We got off the exit within a block of the place. We were less than a mile away when we heard gunshots. I pulled the car over to the side of the road. I tried to see through my windshield what was going on. Neither one of us could see a thing. The rain was too heavy.

I reached for the antique .45 I had my pocket before I remembered that the goons had taken it from me and given it to Davis.

The rain let up a little bit, and thanks to the help of my wiper blades, I was able to see fully clothed men and half-naked women running to their cars. They were getting inside and pulling away as fast as they could. I got out of my car and walked around to the passenger side of the vehicle where Mia was still sitting. I opened up the door and rolled down the window to see if I could get a better view. I was using the passenger side door as a shield in case any bullets came flying my way. I asked Mia to reach into the glove compartment hand me the small pair of binoculars I kept there.

She did as I asked.

Putting them to my eyes, the only thing I could see through them were the lights on top of the squad cars. There was one other vehicle in the parking lot, and I knew in a heartbeat that it didn't belong to the police: a black Cadillac

SUV. It must have been moved to the front once Mia and I had left the premises.

Two men crawled into it. One of them was Dustin, and the other one was Davis.

I watched as the car pulled out of the parking lot and head in our direction. I threw my arms around Mia before pulling her out of the car and onto the ground. She screamed at the top of her lungs, and I screamed at the top of mine, "Get down!" I knew my trench coat would protect her from both the rain and the mud, but not from the bullets. I threw myself on top of her before I used my hands to cover her face and eyes.

There were two gunshots. One of the bullets hit my windshield, and the other hit my passenger side door. The next sound I heard was a loud thud on the top of my car. Something bounced off the roof of my vehicle and hit me in the back. It was the antique .45, and it was out of bullets. I got off the ground only to look back and see the black SUV still driving away with Davis hanging out of one of the windows screaming profanities at me.

Mia groaned as if she had just woken up from a bad night's sleep.

Picking her up off the ground, I asked her if she was okay.

She nodded. "Other than being cold, dirty, and wet, I'm all right."

She cocked her head back to see that the back of my trench coat was now completely covered in mud, yet again. She turned her back and opened the trench coat to see what had become of her white, skimpy outfit.

People who were driving by us must've thought she was flashing me.

I pulled the two ends of the trench coat back together. "Stay here," I ordered her before adjusting my porkpie hat.

"Oh, hell no," she protested as her bare feet chased after me. "I'm coming with you." She held onto the trench coat as tight as she could so the now soft rain wouldn't hit her body.

"You're going to die of pneumonia," I yelled, not looking back to face her.

"Better than bleeding to death from gunshot wounds," she screamed through the thunder before adding, "if they come back."

She had a point, and it made me walk even faster.

We opened the door to the building, and we were greeted by two cops holding guns. I threw my arms up in the air, "Detective Josh Slim, Rockford PD."

They let me go, but they stopped Mia.

"She's with me," I told the two men.

They looked confused but let Mia through anyway.

"Where's Chief Cook?" I asked one of the officers in the room. He had been checking out the goons lying on the ground to see if any of them were still alive.

She pointed towards the back at two policemen who were kneeling next to Chief Cook where he lay, near the room we had left Davis and his henchman in.

"Chief!" I screamed.

Mia and I knelt next to his body along with the two other officers who were there.

"He doesn't have much time," one of them told me. "They shot his chest. It was a perfect hit, right where the body armor didn't cover."

"Slim," the chief said as he pointed at me.

"You stupid fool," I said to him, "I warned you not to take on Davis by yourself."

"I didn't," he coughed. "I got a posse together, and we rushed him just like a bunch of cowboys."

"I tried to warn you."

"You did."

Tears began to form in Mia's eyes.

"Are you one of Davis's girls or, are you an angel?" the dying man asked the girl next to me.

"I'm Mia Quarry," my client said with pride.

"Oh," he said before coughing again.

He then gave Mia something she never thought she would receive from anyone in a million years: An apology. "I'm sorry for what my daughter did to you."

The tears left Mia's eyes and rolled down her cheeks.

"Slim," the dying man called for my attention, "take care of Jennifer like you took care of your client."

Those were the last orders I received from Chief Peter Cook.

Chapter 18

The rain may have washed Mia's tears away but not my anger. I was red, redder than that silly red camel hair sport coat Davis had been wearing, but I knew I had to bottle it up and stick it on a shelf for Mia's sake. I offered to carry her back to my car, but she insisted on walking. As we walked, she told me that after what had just transpired and seeing how brave Chief Cook was going in there at full speed, she felt she now had the courage to go home and tell her parents the truth. When we got back to my car the first thing she did was pull out her cell phone from her purse and send a text.

"Who are you texting?" I asked.

"Troy," she said with a smile as she played with the device, "I think it will be much easier if I told the three most important people in my life what I've been doing at the same time."

I gave her a ride back home.

She took off my mud-soaked trench coat before she dug her street clothes out of her oversized purse.

I continued to stare at the road. I forced my eyes to stay focused on the cars in front of me and not look at the eighteen-year-old girl who was putting on her jeans and t-shirt next to me.

After my car came to a stop at her mailbox, she took one last look at the bullet hole in my windshield and asked me, "Is it legal for you to drive like this?"

"Not really," I said, cracking a smile, "but tonight, cops will be more concerned with drivers who have headlights out than people who have bullet holes in their windshield."

She rolled her eyes as she opened her car door. "Have a good night, Mister Slim."

"You too, kid," I said to her as I watched her run up her driveway with her high-heeled platform shoes in one hand and oversized purse in the other. "You're gonna need it," I whispered before pulling away from the edge of her driveway.

I headed straight for the police department. I did a bad thing and checked my cell phone while driving. I received a text from Sergeant Joey Daniels. The text was only four words long, "Cook has been shot."

When I finally arrived, the department was a mess. It looked like casual Friday, and bring-your-child-to-work-day fell on the same day at an insane asylum. I decided to be a professional.

I went straight into Cook's office and shut the door. The blinds were still closed from the last time we were in his office. I flipped open the laptop, turned it on, and sent a message to Erika Sin. I typed a few choice words before adding, "Did you honestly think you could get away with this? You want to get away, now I'm giving you your chance. You run as fast as you can because now you have every cop in two states hunting you down for the murder of Chief Peter Cook. I dare you to try to get away. Just try it."

I waited for a response, but nothing came back to me. I dug my fingernails into the chief's desk before I pounded on it with my fist. After three minutes, I gave up and walked out the door for a breather.

I was halfway down the hallway when Sergeant Daniels caught me. "Slim," he said before running to catch up with me.

"Joey, I know you're upset."

"We're all upset. Every man we've got from here to the state line is ready to go after Davis. Some already have."

"And I'm about to join them."

He tried to talk some sense into me. "You're not thinking about taking down Davis all by yourself, are you?" His question brought on deja-vu of the similar conversation I'd had with the chief.

"I had the opportunity to do it a few hours ago."

"What are you talking about?"

I told him briefly how I had gone there alone and that Davis and his goons denied killing Melanie. I also told him how they threw me out of there. I left out all the parts about Mia.

Joey always believed everything happened for a reason, and he continued to try to reason with me. "But, Slim, if you had done that, you would have been killed."

"Better me than a family man. He had a wife and a daughter. He had a house, a career, and at least twenty more years of this life and this job before a cozy retirement. Now, instead, he's dead, and an old fart like me is still alive."

"You can't blame yourself for that."

"No," I told him. "But, I can blame someone else."

Another officer from the Rockford Police Department distracted my friend; the distraction was all the opportunity I needed to make it back to the office.

I checked the computer once again and had received a message from Erika Sin.

They had typed back three words to me, "Bring it on."

Those three words were all I needed to see. I pulled out the top desk drawer where the chief had kept his bullets. I reloaded the antique .45, put the gun in my suit coat pocket, and walked out the door.

Before I could make it out of the building, my old friend stopped me again. "Just where do you think you're going?" He saw the slight bulge coming from the pocket of my suit coat. "You really are going to try to take Davis down alone, aren't you?"

"Well, why shouldn't I?"

"You saw what just happened to the guys who went after him. Those were men far younger than you, and they had bigger guns than the one you're carrying now. You're not in your prime anymore."

"Neither is he."

"That may be true, but he's been putting the moves on us for years now. I hate to say it, but Davis is quick."

"My gun is quick!" I shouted at him before I stormed out of the building. I got in my car and headed to see the one person I had to see before going on a crazy suicide mission, my brother.

Chapter 19

I rang the doorbell of the rectory four times before my brother answered. He opened the door and was surprised by my appearance. "Josh, you are soaking wet. Where is your coat?"

"I gave it to a stripper," I said without missing a beat.

He shot me a confused look before asking, "Why do I get the feeling you're telling me the truth?"

I shook the rain from my hat and walked through the door and into the building he called home.

He didn't say a word as I walked past him. Instead, he just stood there and waited for me to speak.

So, I spoke. "Look, I just came here to say goodbye."

I was confusing him even more. "Goodbye? Where are you going?"

"I'm going to hunt down Danny Davis," I told him without going into any details as to why.

"I've heard you talk about this Davis character before," he said with that great, brotherly concern. "From what you've told me, he's an extremely dangerous character."

"Indeed, he is."

"What do you think your chances of survival are?"

"Survival? Zero."

"Why are you doing this?" he asked me as he shook his head from side to side.

"He killed Chief Peter Cook tonight."

"My word." My brother crossed himself.

Instead of giving him the full story, I summed everything up in a simple sentence. "Davis shot him in the chest, Jacob. I was right there when he died."

"So, why are you going after him by yourself?"

I gave my brother one reason and one word, "Vengeance."

"Vengeance is mine, saithe The Lord." Of course, I should have known he was going to quote Scripture.

"Yeah, well, where is that in The Bible?"

My brother thought for a moment. "Deuteronomy chapter thirty-two, verse thirty-five. If I remember correctly, and it can also be found in Romans chapter twelve, verse nineteen. If I remembered it correctly."

I looked back at him and called him something he hated being called, "Smartass."

A small giggle left his mouth. It was a familiar giggle, one he used to do whenever I got into trouble, and he didn't. Then, he informed me, "That'll cost you one Hail Mary."

"What about for all the other stuff?"

"You've never told me about the other stuff. You've been holding all of it in for years. But I'm pretty sure after I hear all about the other stuff, your penance would be a rosary each night for the rest of your life."

"I thought I couldn't come to you for Confession," I said, reminding him of one of our previous conversations.

"Given the present circumstances," he said before bouncing his head back and forth, "I think the bishop would forgive me."

"You aren't going to try to stop me," I asked, ready for a fight.

"Josh," he said before he patted me on the back. "You've been able to outwrestle me ever since I could walk. Now come on, let me hear your Confession so I can give you your penance of praying one rosary each night for the rest of your life."

"How long does it take to get through one of those?"

He shrugged his shoulders, "Twenty minutes, maybe a half-hour, tops."

I smiled back at him. "Oh, trust me, if I make it through this, I will be more than happy to give The Blessed Mother thirty minutes of my life every night.

What I thought was going to take five simple minutes, instead, took a full twenty-five. As soon as we were done, my brother asked me, "Would you like something to drink before you go?"

"No," I said to him looking around the room for my coat before remembering I'd left that muddy ball of cloth in the car. "You have already stalled me enough as it is." I turned my head to see an open door leading to a small room with a toilet inside it. "But I would like to use the bathroom if I could before I go?"

"Certainly," he said as he reached his hand out as if he was introducing me to the bathroom. "Be my guest." I went inside and did my business, but when I went to leave and turned the doorknob, the door wouldn't open. The door itself was jammed. "Hey, what gives," I shouted at the inanimate object.

"I'm not letting you out of there, Josh. I'm not letting you out of there for your own good."

"Jacob, you're crazy. I have to get going. I have to find Davis."

"You're retired. You should let the cops who are being paid to handle it, handle it."

"I am being paid to handle it," I yelled through the door, "and if you don't let me out, I'll break this door down, or I will shoot the handle off with my gun."

"There's a chair in front of it. I'd like to see you shoot that too."

I did a quick search around the enclosed space to see if there was another way out. There wasn't. "What are you going to do?" I questioned him through the door. "Keep me in here for the rest of my life?"

"You have a bathroom, and you have water," he said, almost as if he was teasing me. "Tomorrow is my day off, and I can slip food to you through the bottom of the door. I don't have to be anywhere until Tuesday morning at seven o'clock."

"What about school? What about the students?" I asked, trying to trip him up.

"It's the last week of school. They will be fine without me. If a situation arises where one of the students need last rites or something, I'm pretty confident one of the other priests at the school can handle it."

I looked around the bathroom, trying to see if there was anything flat enough that I could shove underneath the door. There wasn't, but there was a shower curtain. I took the thin shower curtain rod and started breaking it into pieces, making sure I had at least one long piece to slide underneath the door. Once I had a piece that was long enough, I looked underneath the door and was able to see one of the legs of the chair. I lined a long piece of the shower curtain rod up carefully with the back right leg of the chair. I carefully aimed the cheap piece of plastic before standing and pushing it underneath the door with my foot. "Bullseye," I whispered to myself. I had hit the chair leg on the first try.

When I opened the bathroom door, there was my brother, holding a gun in his hand.

"I can't let you go, Josh." He was shaking. He was nervous.

"Have you ever fired that thing?" I asked him as I slowly raised my hands in the air.

"A few times," he confessed to me, still shaking. "After all, with all of these school shootings going around, one has to be prepared. I'm going to tell you, dear brother, it is very easy to conceal a weapon underneath a cassock."

I inspected the weapon as best I could. "You went out and bought a gun. I'm very proud of you, brother. Tell me, is it even loaded?"

"More loaded than you think." He held it even tighter and raised it. The gun was now at my eye level. It was as if he was proud of himself for being able to defend himself in any situation. But based on the way I knew his brain worked, my guess was, he thought he was protecting me more than defending himself.

"Are you really going to shoot me, Jacob?"

"If that's what it takes to stop you from going after Davis, then yes." He waved the gun in the air and pointed it towards the kitchen before he returned it to its original position.

I walked into the kitchen as he had instructed me using his nonverbal skills.

He leaned his back on the kitchen counter before he spoke to me again. "Now, you are going to sit down at the kitchen table, and I am going to make us both a fresh pot of coffee, and we are both going to stay up and talk all night long if we have to."

"Are you sure you're able to stay up all night, Jacob? You've always been an early bird, and I've always been a night owl."

"I've stayed up past my bedtime on many occasions. After all, I do get many phone calls in the middle of the night from parishioners asking me to come over to their house or the hospital to give their loved one's last rites." He continued to hold the gun at me. He kept his eyes on me, only taking them off me for a brief moment just to grab something out of the cupboard before focusing them back on me.

I had to give him credit. He knew how to keep a hostage at bay. The only problem was I knew what to do to get myself out of the situation.

He put two coffee cups on the table and asked me to choose whichever one I liked. One of the mugs was the one I had gotten him as a birthday gift before he had left to be a pastor for three Catholic churches out in Galena. I grabbed the one with the least sentimental value just in case I had to break it over his head. I held it close to me, keeping both hands on the mug and the handle pointed at my chest. I use my left foot to hook the leg of his chair, and I pulled it closer toward me. Lastly, I pushed my chair out a bit from the table. I was setting him up, and he didn't even know it.

As soon as the coffee was finished brewing, he walked over to the kitchen table. The gun was in his right hand, and the coffee pot was in his left. "Now," he instructed me, "raise the coffee cup up, and I will pour you a drink."

I raised my coffee cup into the air, making sure that my left hand was higher than his right.

He started to pour and when he did, I let go of the mug. Then I grabbed his right hand with my left, and forced his arm behind his back. I put my right forearm on the back of his neck and whispered in his ear, "Drop it, drop it."

He dropped the gun to the floor and laid the coffee pot gently on the table. I picked the gun up and yelled at him, "You shouldn't have done that, Jacob. You shouldn't have."

He started to quiver. "I was trying to save your life, Josh. Do you blame me?"

I was practically foaming at the mouth. "The only thing I blame you for is wasting my time." I kept the gun on him, making sure he wasn't going to go for it.

"Are you really going to shoot me, Josh?"

"If that's what it takes to stop you from trying to prevent me from going after Davis, then yes."

He smiled at me. Tears began to form in his eyes. "Take my coat," he said. His voice was cracking. "It's pretty bad out there, and you seem to have lost yours."

"Thanks," I said before I took the heavy, thick, black coat off the coat rack that was next to the door. I put it slowly around my body, making sure I didn't take the gun off my own brother, even though there really wasn't a need to. After all, he was still in the kitchen and about twenty feet away from me.

As I turned around to open the door, he called out to me, "Josh, I love you." When I turned to look back at him, tears were pouring down his cheeks.

"I love you too," I said to him, tears forming in my own eyes. I closed the door to the rectory, leaving him in there all alone. I walked to my car with the mission to find Danny Davis, along with the realization that I might have just seen my brother for the last time.

Chapter 20

Danny Davis may have had his business in Wisconsin, but both his home and hideout were in Illinois. He planned it this way so that if any of the boys in blue in Wisconsin were giving him trouble, he could easily do his business across the state line without anyone up north knowing. It was a smart move, but it wasn't a smart move when he killed an Illinois police officer. I naturally assumed the SWAT team was on their way to his home in South Beloit. I decided to head to a storage unit facility that I knew Davis and his men had nicknamed Complex Ninety, here in Rockford.

They gave the storage unit that stupid nickname because their storage unit number was ninety. Yeah, as if we, the authorities, couldn't figure that out. The storage unit itself was located in the nine-hundred block of Ninth Street. It was quite impressive as far as storage units go. The place itself took up almost a full four acres of land. The first one-hundred storage units were large enough to park a pickup truck and a boat inside of them. The remaining storage units were only big enough to fit a four-door vehicle and a compact car inside of them.

If Davis was hiding in his storage unit, I knew I would need a small bomb in order to break down the door. I stopped at a gas station. I bought a gas can, some fuel to go inside of it, and some fireworks, which they conveniently had.

"Aren't you guys selling these a bit early?" I asked the clerk.

"Merchandise moves slowly around here," he said, chewing on something in his mouth. Then he told me his boss gets them in during the first week of May, and they keep ordering them until after the Fourth of July. The stuff out in front for customers to see was just some they put out for the parents to buy when they were in a jam or for their kids. He then told me, "If you want the good stuff, we keep it behind the counter."

"Good stuff?" I asked. Now the kid had my attention.

He told me his boss makes a road trip up to Wisconsin the moment the cheap stuff comes in. Then he repeated himself, telling me how the stuff out there was for the parents, but it was also out there as a tease to get customers asking if they had anything more powerful. I asked him if they did, and he said, "We do," before he explained how and why it was kept behind the counter. He warned me that the stuff behind the counter was almost triple the price of the stuff out front. After finishing his long-winded explanation, he asked me, "Are you interested in fireworks, mister?"

"Indeed, I am," I smiled at the boy, nodding.

He showed me what he had. It wasn't going to blow up a door by itself, but it was going to get the job done more than the stuff they had on display would have.

I bought everything he had behind the counter.

I loaded up my car and drove straight to the gate of the storage facility. The place required a code to get in. Although it had been raining a lot lately, I had an idea. I searched around, managing to find some dirt that was still dry on the ground below the cover over the area where the keypad was. I grabbed some and rubbed a little bit in between my hands.

Using all of the air I could muster from my lungs; I blew the dirt from my hands into the air and towards the keypad. After it was on there, I shined my flashlight on the nine-digit device, and thanks to the handy little light-making machine I always kept in my car, I was able to see the fingerprints on the buttons people had pushed the most. There were only three buttons with fingerprints on them; the one, the eight, and the nine. My first logical conclusion was someone had set the code to someone's birth year. So, I tried nineteen-eighteen first, and what do you know, it worked.

The gate pulled back, and I drove my car right inside the row of oversized garages with ease. I turned my lights off and let my car roll by itself till I was closer to storage unit number ninety. I got out of my car and began my work.

After seeing light piercing through the cracks, I had every reason to believe both Davis and his faithful henchman were inside. I grabbed some duct tape I had in the trunk of my car. I quietly used it to line and hold the fireworks in place against the door. Once I finished, I poured some gasoline on the ground. If the fireworks wouldn't motivate them to move out, I would smoke them out.

After pouring the flammable liquid on the ground, I took my brother's gun, and I fired a few shots into the air. "This is Slim," I yelled at the garage door, "Open up, or I'm coming in." I lit the fireworks and ran behind my car for protection. The oversized bottle rockets exploded like crazy. As soon as they were done, I fired a few more bullets with my brother's gun. This time, instead of shooting the air, I shot at the door.

The door to the storage unit lifted and rose just a little bit off the ground.

I lit a few smoke bombs and rolled them under the door to the storage unit.

"You've gotta do better than that, Slim," said a voice on the other side of the door. A few shots came from the other side of the garage door.

My strategy was working, and I stuck with it. I repeated the process by throwing more smoke bombs underneath the door. After repeating the process, a third time, the door rose up and there were two people firing bullets through the multicolored smoke.

I fired a few shots before I came out from behind my car and rushed towards the door. I started firing like crazy.

When the smoke cleared, Dustin's body was on the ground. The blood from his wounds slowly leaked from his body onto the expensive black suit he wore. It seemed he had climbed a tower of boxes and tried to shoot at me from there, but it hadn't worked. I don't know what killed him first, the bullets to his chest or the fall, but I knew one thing: the big man was dead.

Danny Davis was still alive, but barely. He was lying on his stomach, grumbling but not moving. It appeared as though he had tried the same strategy as Dustin, but instead of shooting him in the torso, I had mostly put holes in his legs.

I rolled him over, so he could face me. I screamed at him, "You maniac, you crazy maniac!"

He laughed as if it were some sort of joke. "Funny, I was about to say the same thing to you." He coughed up some blood, and it was then I noticed I had managed to get one of my shots into his chest. He started talking again, "It looks like you picked up a few things from me. I have to give you credit. It looks like you finally got me. After all this time, you finally got me."

"I didn't get you," I said as I stood above him. "You brought this on yourself. All I did was respond to your challenge. After all, you did say, 'Bring it on'."

"When did I say that?"

I was confused. "You mean, you're not Erika Sin?"

He was laughing and coughing up blood at the same time. "Who's Erika Sin?"

"Wasn't that the alias you were using to talk to me online?"

"I never chatted with you online, but I can promise you this, I will chat with you in the afterlife." He gave me a wink and a smile before he finally died.

Within a minute, a dozen squad cars were inside the storage facility. The bodies of Danny Davis and his henchman Dustin were taken to the morgue in ambulances even though the drivers openly admitted they wanted to dump the bodies in the river.

We started to open the boxes stored in the unit. We found everything from business ledgers to pornographic material. Most of the boxes had cash in them, but there was one box, in particular, all of us were fascinated by.

"What is it?" one of the officers asked, confused by what we had just found.

I grabbed the first file in the box and flipped through it. "These are the names and faces of the girls Davis was trying to sell to his big-money clients."

"So, he was running a human trafficking ring after all."

"Save this box for me, will you? I have to see if my Jane Doe is somewhere in there."

"Yes, sir," the officer said before taking it somewhere. Wherever he took it, I still, to this day, don't know where that box ended up, and neither does he.

I let the third shifters clean up the mess I had made. Instead of joining them in the celebration, I walked back to my car.

Someone shouted to me, "Hey, Slim, where are you going?"

"Back to headquarters," I yelled back, "I have some business I need to take care of."

Chapter 21

The moment I got back to the station, I was greeted with pats on the back and people telling me what a great job I had done. I ignored it all and headed straight for the chief's office. I opened the laptop. As it was booting up, I pulled out my cell phone and noticed I had a few missed calls and a couple of texts from Alex. I called him back.

"Slim, praise Jesus! For a moment, I thought you were dead. Listen, I have something important to tell you."

I cut Alex off in the middle of his excitement. "Before you do, I have something important to ask. Is there a way to track where an instant message comes from?"

"That's what I've been trying to tell you this whole time. There is a way you can find out where the message was sent from."

I really didn't want to drive all the way back to his house. "Do I have to be there with you, or can you just walk me through it over the phone?"

He held his breath for a second. "It's a little bit complicated. You should probably bring the laptop back to me."

I peeked through the blinds to see people standing outside of the office. "Uh, I really can't do that, Alex."

"Why not?"

I moved away from the door and back to the desk. "I'm in the chief of police's office with the laptop, and I really shouldn't remove it from here."

"Why? Is he there?"

"Uh, no."

"Is he coming back?"

"Uh, not anytime soon."

"Then what's stopping you, Slim? In the past, you would just take what you wanted and deal with the consequences later. Why have you changed all of a sudden?"

He was starting to piss me off, "Because the dead girl who once owned this laptop was the daughter of the chief of police, and now he's dead. I'm trying to find his daughter's killer while everyone is celebrating the death of who they all thought the killer was. Plus, I am trying to leave all of the evidence right where it is. To top it all off, in less than a minute or two, there will be officers who will walk in here to start cleaning this place up. If they find me in here, things are going to get really awkward really fast."

I kept talking, but he kept repeating himself, "Okay, okay, okay, I get the picture." He took a deep breath before continuing. "The easiest way to do this is for you just to stay put."

"That's better," I thought to myself.

"I'm going to walk you through changing the password on her social media account as well as the phone number linked to the account first, and we'll go from there."

"Make it quick," I said still using my frustrated tone of voice.

He walked me through every step of the process.

I did every step he mentioned as quickly as I could.

No sooner had I finish did he tell me, "Now, get the heck out of there. The rest I can easily walk you through. All you will have to do is use your phone."

I peeked out the blinds once more, and I waited till no one was in sight before I snuck out of the office. Once I was out, I resumed my conversation with Alex. "Okay, I'm in the hallway, what am I going to do next?"

"I know how you are with technology, Slim, so it would be best if you take me off the phone so that you can fully focus on downloading these apps. Is there a public phone you can use in the building?"

"Yeah," I told him as I made a grin with my mouth that showed off a few of my teeth. "I know just the place."

I hung up and walked to the clerk's office. Behind the desk sat a five-foot two-inch woman whose short light brown hair barely went past her mason jar thick glasses. The heavy lenses themselves were held in place by the heavy thick brown plastic frames that almost matched her hair color perfectly. Her name tag said Michelle, but everyone called her "Short Shelley." I called out her name and forced her to raise those ten-pound spectacles up to my level.

"Hey, Slim, how's it going?"

"It's been a good day and a bad day," I said, using my flirting voice.

"I bet," she said, flirting back with me, "but you got him, Slim, and that's all that matters."

I tried my hardest to go along with it even though I knew Melanie's killer was still out there. "Yeah, that's true."

"So," she took off her glasses and fixed her hair before asking me, "what can I do for you?"

I pulled out a piece of paper from my pocket. "This was the last thing Chief Cook gave to me before he died. We were working on a case together."

She put her glasses back on and became businesslike again. "Well, this was very generous of him. I'm going to have to get some approval before I cut this."

"Not a problem, but while you're gone, would you mind if I used the phone?"

"As long as you're not calling another woman," she winked at me before bending her knee to pop her heel up in the air, "then sure."

As soon as she was gone, I picked up the phone and called Alex.

He answered, "Thank you for calling Sites by Alex. This is Alex. How may I help you?"

"Alex, it's Slim. Is that how you answer the phone every time a number you don't know calls?"

"Well yeah, Slim. You've known me for all these years, and you still don't know the name of my business?"

"I guess it wasn't that important for you to tell me," I said sarcastically before I got serious. "Look, just tell me what I need to do. I'm on a time crunch here."

"Okay, first, I need you to go into your app store and download three different apps. I'll give you them one at a time."

I did as he instructed. I must've said, "Alright," to him fifty times over the phone.

"Okay, since you are done downloading, I will need you to keep all three apps open all at the same time."

"Is my phone capable of doing that?" I asked with uncertainty in my voice. Hell, I didn't know how all this new technology worked.

"Yes!" he shouted.

My next question was more serious than my first one. "Am I capable of doing that?"

Alex growled a bit before mentioning, "This is why I wanted you here."

The door behind me was opening. "People are coming into the office. I have to go. Bye. Thanks again, Alex. You're a genius." I hung up the phone and stuffed my cell phone back into my pocket.

When I turned around, Shelly was standing there, and behind her were two men who really didn't care for me. Their names were Kyle Bennet and Reggie Rodriguez. They were two detectives, who I knew didn't like the fact that an old fart like me kept beating them to the punch on multiple occasions.

"Hello, boys," I said to the two of them as they stood there looking like bodyguards protecting the loveable Short Shelly, "what can I do for you two?"

Bennet spoke first. "We couldn't help but notice how Chief Cook's last request was for you to receive a check."

"Well, I'm glad to see you figured something out on your own for once in your life. As a matter of fact, yes, he wanted to see that I got paid for my work. I worked with him on his last case."

"Very interesting, considering he died only a few hours ago. You know, Slim, you may have been the guy to take down Davis, but that doesn't give you the right to capitalize on the chief's death."

I was starting to get hot. "What are you trying to say, Kyle?"

"I'm trying to say I think after the hero stunt you pulled, you left the scene to come back here and write yourself your own paycheck." He held up the piece of paper I had handed to Shelley just before she left the room. "Tell us, is this how much you think you should be rewarded for taking out the boss's killer?"

"Look at the signature," I pointed to the note he was holding in the air. "Do you really think I could forge the man's signature that well, with these hands?" I held up my hand to show its age and how unsteady it had become over time. "Better yet, do you really think I could forge the signature of a man I met only two days ago?"

"You might be right, but we both still have a lot of questions for you, amigo," Rodriguez mentioned to me before the door opened behind him.

Head Detective Carlson stepped into the room to save me from all the accusations. "What's going on here, boys?

"It seems there's a bit of confusion around here," I started to explain. "Before Chief Cook and his suicide squad went on their crusade, he wanted to make sure I got paid for solving the case of his daughter's murder. Bennet and Rodriguez here think I went ahead and cut my own paycheck after the whole debacle ended."

"Is that so? May I see the note?"

Bennet handed Carlson the note.

"I don't see anything wrong with this," Carlson said after looking over the check. He passed the note to Shelly. "But, I think it's time the truth came out."

"I agree," Bennet said, snarling.

Carlson waved for Bennet, Rodriguez, and Shelly to move out of the way so that he could lean comfortably against the door. He gave the two detectives the same look dog owners give their puppies when they pee on the rug. "You two remember the body we found in the river on Friday night? Well, that wasn't some Jane Doe. That was the body of Chief Cook's daughter Melanie."

Both of their mouths dropped to the ground.

Carlson continued to talk. "Chief Cook hired Slim here to solve the case because of my recommendation. While working on the case, Slim discovered that Danny Davis was buying nude videos the chief's daughter and other girls were making of themselves. Davis planned to sell the videos online for a quick buck. The ones he liked, he would hire into his club, and the ones he especially liked he would sell to his high-paying customers. Am I right, Slim?"

"So far, so good."

"Slim reported all this back to Chief Cook, and the man took matters into his own hands. I know all of this because I was one of the men, he had asked to go in with him during his raid on Naughty-or-Nice. I can only assume Slim here went on the raid as well. He seems to be the only man who has come back from those who went inside the club so far." There was a sense of sadness in his voice. He was almost sure everyone inside had died during the raid. Biting his lip, he turned to me and asked, "Am I right, Slim?"

I didn't want to disagree with a man defending me in front of two people who had just accused me of forgery. So, I simply repeated, "So far, so good."

"Alright, listen, both of you. If everything you two say is true, then why were the blinds shut in the office?" Rodriguez asked.

"The chief did that himself to make sure no one would interrupt us while I showed him what was on his daughter's laptop." I answered, trying to be patient with the two buffoons and their questions.

"Then, why did people tell us they saw you coming out of the chief's office just recently?"

"I was checking to make sure the laptop was still there. Why? What do you think I was doing? Writing a check to myself?"

Bennet growled at me before asking, "Alright, show us this laptop."

I walked the three men down to the chief's office. Shelly stayed behind. I flipped the lights on and showed them where the laptop was. "There you are, boys. It's right where I left it."

Bennet opened it up and did nothing at first but stare into the black mirror. "How are we supposed to get into this?"

"My computer guy changed the password to my last name. All lower case." I said before I pulled out from the fat file Cook once threw at me. "Here it is, boys, everything you need. A whole file on Davis composed of information collected over the past year by Former Chief Rawson, Chief Cook, and myself. Between this file and that computer, you three should be able to put everything together."

Bennet shut the violet and black laptop he had picked up off the desk. "Rawson, Cook, and you all working on the same case? I can hardly believe it."

"Well, in case none of you do," I said, going on to explain to them I'd had my computer guy make sure all of Melanie Cook's passwords were changed so I could easily access her socials. I told them what we had found should still be saved. They would be able to log in and pull up through a conversation between Davis and me. I mentioned that Davis had used the alias Erika Sin to communicate with the girls at the high school and to get them to send him nude pictures and videos of themselves. Finally, I told them that Davis had also made threats on both the lives of Jennifer Cook and Mia Quarry.

I told them that I had shown all of it to Chief Cook before he showed me the file on Danny Davis that he and Rawson had worked on after I retired.

"Seems like you wrapped it up pretty good, Slim," Carlson congratulated me. "We will take it from here."

"Are you telling me I can go get my check now?"

Carson looked at Bennet and Rodriguez before giving me the answer. "Of course, you can. In fact, I will even use the office phone right now to call Shelly and tell her, 'It's okay'."

I walked back down the hallway to the clerk's office and got my check from Shelly.

"Sorry, Slim," she said in her sweet soothing voice. "I hope this doesn't affect our relationship." She batted those eyes that were twenty-five years younger than mine at me.

"Shelley, I don't think anything could have an effect on our relationship."

She stretched a smile across that cabbage patch doll face of hers before her face turned as red as the button-down shirt she was wearing. I couldn't help but notice as she unbuttoned the top two buttons of the seductive red shirt. She looked up to see if I had noticed what she was doing before adding, "Well, don't be a stranger."

"I won't," I told her with a smile before I walked out of the building.

I had only taken two steps on the sidewalk before pulling out my phone to take a look at the apps Alex had told me to download. I wanted to make sure Davis wasn't lying to me. But in all honesty, I couldn't think of a good reason why a dying man would want to make his last words a lie. I stood there like a statue in the parking lot, checking my phone. I couldn't believe I was behaving like a fifteen-year-old girl. When the address came up, I blinked twice in disbelief at the location it was showing me.

Five seconds later, Alex's name popped up the screen. He was calling me. "Slim, did you download the apps correctly? Did you get the address?"

"Oh, I got it alright," I informed him. I knew the address all too well.

Chapter 22

I arrived at the address where the message had supposedly come from. I rang the doorbell twice before a beautiful woman answered the door. "Why, Josh, what a surprise."

"Hello, Jennifer," I said to her.

"Won't you come in?"

I did just as she said, only this time, I didn't take off my shoes.

I followed her past the family room and into the kitchen, where two tall candles were lit on a table. Adjacent to each candle was a placemat, and on top of the placemats were the fanciest dishes I had ever seen in my life. I knew they had to be expensive just by how they looked, even in the candlelight.

"Dinner for two?" I asked, pointing to the fancy silverware on the table.

Whatever she had planned, it was going to be a romantic evening. She was wearing a jet-black robe that was as dark as the rest of her house. I could see nothing underneath it except the two black stiletto shoes that barely covered her feet. The tips of her toes were sticking out of the stilettos, and two black straps wrapped themselves around her toes just above the nails. I walked around her and noticed one of the heels had a crack in it. Much like the crack in her voice as she answered my question. "All of this is for Pete. I thought the two of us could use a romantic evening together after all the hard work he's been doing searching for Melanie."

"How thoughtful of you," I said before coming back around to face her.

"How do you like my hair?" she asked, turning her back on me. "I worked really hard on it." Her gorgeous, curled blonde hair almost hit me in the face like the bottom of the thin jet-black robe hit me in my kneecaps.

"Listen, Jennifer," I said, fighting for her attention as she faced me again, "I hate to be the one to break this to you, but I figured it was better I did than anyone else. Pete's dead."

She began to cry instantly. "I knew it! What other reason would you be here for other than to break more bad news to me?"

"I'm sorry, but as I said, I wanted you to hear it from me first before you found out from anyone else."

She turned around and faced me. "How did it happen?"

I didn't want to tell her while standing up. "Sit down, Jennifer. It's time I told you the truth about everything."

"I prefer to stand."

"Suit yourself. This is going to be a long story, and you're not going to like it."

"Try me!" She braced herself by crossing her arms and resting them on top of her two big voluptuous breasts.

"Fine," I said before stuffing my hands back into the still mud-covered trench coat I had finally decided to put back on myself. "Friday night, two of Melanie's classmates, Troy Dublin and Mia Quarry, found Melanie's dead body floating in The Rock River. After much investigation, it was believed that the person who murdered Melanie was Danny Davis, a strip club owner in Beloit, Wisconsin. Pete got a posse of men together, and they went after Davis. Unfortunately, Davis was prepared for their arrival."

Even though the room was dark except for the two lit, candles I could see her face turning red with fury. "Let me guess. When Pete went after Davis, he got killed."

I nodded.

"Where is Davis now?" she pouted.

"I killed him."

"You're lying to me." she shot back at me. "Just like you've lied to me about everything. You knew the entire time Melanie was dead, and you didn't tell me a single word about it."

"I'm sorry, Jennifer, but your husband didn't want anyone finding out about Melanie's death until after the case was closed."

"Let me make another guess. It was 'police business,'" she said, making quotation marks with her fingers in the air. "Those were the words Pete always used whenever I asked about anything going on in his work. He would always say it was 'police business.'"

"I'm sorry, Jennifer, I really am."

"The only thing I'm sorry about was sleeping with you last night. I was sorry about it the moment I came back into this house. Now, I'm even sorrier about it after finding out everything you have told me from the beginning was a lie." She pointed her finger down the dark hallway before growling. "There's the door, see yourself out."

"I can't do that, Jennifer."

She laughed at me. "What are you going to do, Josh? Are you going to rape me in my own home?" She opened her jet-black paper-thin robe to reveal her naked body to me. She held onto it and stretched it out as far as it would go as if she were making wings to fly away from me and the whole situation. "Go ahead, Detective Slim! Go ahead and do me right here, right now. I'll even scream for you if you'd like. Just like I'll scream for the press tomorrow morning." She let out a sinister laugh revealing a little bit of her craziness before continuing. "Can you imagine it, Josh? Hero detective rapes dead cop's wife, now trending!"

"I'm not here to rape you," I growled back at her before telling her my full intentions. "I'm here to arrest you."

"What?" she asked seconds before she closed her robe to hide herself.

"You heard me. I'm here to arrest you for the murder of your own daughter."

"Josh," she started to make her voice crack. "What makes you think I killed my own daughter? How could you accuse me of such a thing?"

"There's an app for that." I pulled out my phone and lit up the screen in the dark room. "I was able to get a hold of Melanie's laptop, but you already knew I had it. Not just because it was missing from her bedroom, but also because I logged on and made a post I wasn't supposed to. You saw it, and you messaged me using the name Erika Sin. A fake profile you've had set up and have been using for a while now. You tried to get me to look the other way. When it didn't work, you threatened to do harm to yourself, which forced me to come here. The man on the deck wasn't some mobster. It was your own husband."

"This is all a lie!" She turned away from me and shoved her hands into the jet-black garment.

"You knew your husband was dead before I even got here. So, you sent me a message to get my blood boiling. You knew I was on somebody's tail, and you knew it wasn't yours. You figured I would kill the guy before coming here to break the news to you myself. There was just one problem." I lit up my phone again to show her what I had been keeping from her. "See this cute little app? All I have to do is tap the message I want, tap the app, and I can trace the message to the point of origin of where it came from. It just so happens the messages were sent from this address!"

"You still can't convict me!"

"Your phone will!" I screamed back at her, "And so will Melanie's once I find her phone in this house."

Fear struck her for a second.

"You didn't throw it in the river with her, did you? Instead, you kept it, and you just threw your daughter in there as naked as she was on the day she came out of you."

"Josh," she said in that sweet soft voice of hers, looking through the flame of the candles into my eyes. "That's a lovely story."

"Well then, why don't you tell me a story?" I growled at her. "Why don't you tell me how Melanie died?"

She took a deep breath before giving me the details. "On Friday night, Melanie and I got into a fight. She slapped me, so I made a fist and hit her back. She fell backward and crashed onto the glass top of our coffee table. Pieces of glass went into her neck. I tried to pull them out as gently as I possibly could without cutting myself, but by the time I had finished, she was dead. She bled to death right on her own living room floor. I knew that if I told Pete what happened, he wouldn't have believed me. Peter tolerated me, but he loved Melanie. She was his little angel. I didn't want to be accused of murdering my own daughter, especially not by my own husband."

"So, you cleaned up the mess?"

"Not before I made a bigger one. I took the baseball bat we have kept in the garage from Melanie's old softball days, and I took a few swings at her to make it look like she was beaten. After making a few marks, I stripped her naked and tied her up with the ropes we used when we moved. I drove out to the river, parked my car on the bridge, got out, and threw her into the water. I seriously thought her body would sink to the bottom, but when she hit the water, I realized too late that the current was too strong. Then, I came back here, and I cleaned up the mess."

"And then Troy and Mia found her."

"That little impoverished bitch. Of all the people in the world to find Melanie, why did it have to be her?"

"Tell me something, why do you and your family hate her so much?"

"Because she did everything in her power to be like my daughter, and she's not. It was Melanie's idea to start taking pictures and videos of herself. It was Melanie's idea to make friends with Danny Davis. It was Melanie's idea to recruit the other girls and bring them to his club. Then that little half-breed bitch showed up at the club one night. Melanie told me about it. The next day, I called Davis and told him to get rid of her. I told him she was a whistleblower. He had a different plan. He was going to let her work at the club for a while. He was going to let her have the attention she so desired, and then, he was going to sell her off like he did with so many other girls I didn't like."

I heard the insinuation that she was more involved with Davis and his business than she let on, but I let it go for the time being.

"But then Melanie came to her defense, didn't she? She defended her, and you two got into a fight. You trained your daughter to be as prejudiced as you were, but when she finally saw the light, she tried to put a stop to your plans.

Jennifer moved her head up and down. Tears were streaming down her face at the same time melted wax was streaming down from the candles. "I only meant to slap Melanie. I didn't mean for her to die." She attempted to walk around the table to get to me, but I moved out of the way. "Josh, you have to believe me."

"I believe Melanie's death was an accident, but I don't think a jury will buy it."

"Why not?"

"You didn't mean to kill your daughter, but the way you handled it caused a lot of people to die, including your own husband. I don't think a jury will let you off so easily. They will still find you guilty of something. Especially when the evidence that you were involved with Davis and human trafficking is brought forward."

She chose to ignore my last comment.

"You're not taking me in, are you, Josh?"

"I have to, Jennifer," I said as I moved around the table to avoid her. "Out of all the news I've given you tonight, that last part is probably the worst of it all."

"But, Josh, you don't have to. Davis is dead, and my husband's own obsession got him killed."

"You knew about his hatred towards Davis, and yet you fed your daughter to that monster anyway?"

"He's not the only detective in the family," she spat back before returning to the subject, "but the case is closed. So many of the high school parents will thank you for what you've done. You can walk away from this a hero. You can walk away from this with me." She opened her robe once again. She let the candlelight gently touch her boobs, illuminating the two luscious round balls of flesh for me to see.

I put my hands in the pockets of my coat and held onto the two guns I had brought in with me, one in each hand. "As tempting as the offer is, I'm sorry, but I can't accept it."

She closed her robe before saying, "Very well then." She pulled out a small gun she had been hiding in one of the pockets of the thin garment and fired at me.

I was ready for it. I turned my body sideways and fired both guns, hoping to startle Jennifer enough to make her drop the weapon.

She ran up the stairs.

I flipped the kitchen table over, spilling everything that was on it. The impact of the table hitting the floor put the candles out immediately.

Jennifer fired two shots in the dark at the wood table, putting cracks into the piece of furniture immediately upon impact.

I realized the table wasn't a safe bet, so I crawled around the table. As I was crawling, I touched two foreign objects, one with my hand and the other one with my knee. It was the fancy dinner plates she had set on the table, still fully intact after my table flip.

"Man, this china is tough," I thought to myself. I picked up the plates so I wouldn't run into them again if I had to crawl around on the floor a second time. I continued my crawl and found myself in the hallway. The upstairs was directly above my head.

Jennifer flipped on a light before screaming at me from above. The angel had now become a demon. "I know where you are, Slim," she's screamed. She thought I was still behind the table. Bullets began to hit the wood.

Once she was out of ammo, I came out of my crouched position to show her where I'd been hiding the whole time. "I'm coming up to get you, Jennifer. I've got two loaded guns. Give up now, and I'll make sure the court goes easy on you."

She scuffed at me. "I tried to surrender to you one time tonight, Josh, and you refused my offer. I'm not doing it a second time." She ran into various rooms upstairs, grabbing pieces of random furniture before coming back to the banister to throw them at me.

I knelt on the ground. Taking my pork pie hat, I slid my favorite piece of headgear on the kitchen floor.

She threw a small lamp at it. Thinking she had made a direct hit, she stopped for a second to observe the damage she had done. If she was going to escape, now was her chance.

If she was going to throw household items at me, I was going to throw one back at her. I took one of the china plates, and using it as a frisbee, threw it at her as she started to come down the stairs. I hit her square in the head.

The cracked heel of the damaged stiletto snapped. Her head landed first on the steps and turned itself in a direction it wasn't supposed to go. She tumbled down the rest of the stairs looking like a big black bouncy ball rolling down a hill. A second or two later, she landed. Her arms and legs were fully stretched, and her robe was fully open, exposing those gorgeous private parts of hers. The stilettos were still on her feet. One perfectly intact, the other with the heel broken just like she was.

"I can't, I can't move, Josh." She screamed in pure terror. "I'm paralyzed. Please help me, Josh."

I shook my head.

"No, we can work out a deal, Josh. I'll even work out a deal with the law. No jury would put a quadriplegic behind bars, would they?"

"I am the jury now!" I spat back at her. "And I, the jury, sentence you to death."

Death was what she deserved. After all, her daughter had looked up to her as if she were a god. Jennifer took advantage of that. When the money ran short because Jennifer couldn't control her own spending, the spending she had tried to blame on her husband, she used Melanie as an offering. She had chosen to sacrifice her own kid on an altar called the internet. When that wasn't enough, she put Melanie into the hands of a god far eviler than you could have possibly imagined. A god that she herself had gotten involved with years before.

Jennifer Cook willingly destroyed her own daughter for the sake of keeping up the lifestyle she wanted her family to live. Choosing to do so instead of being adults and facing bankruptcy for their own sins like she should have. Then when the sacrificial lamb was slaughtered by her own hand, Jennifer Cook attempted to hide the remains in the river. Hoping her daughter would be another unsolved missing person case. Mother Nature, however, had other plans when she allowed Melanie's body to get stuck on the branch of a tree.

So, Mrs. Cook arranged for the blame to be put on the "god" she had sacrificed her daughter to, a man who thought he was God, but in the end, he was turned into a scapegoat. All it costed her were the lives of her loved ones and a few others associated with them.

I looked down at her. My stare was as cold as a Chicago winter, but my anger was hotter than a summer in Mexico. "Why did you do it, Jennifer, why?"

She threw a dumb excuse at me. She told me years ago she had thought about doing some camming and uploading nude videos of herself online, but she didn't believe they would sell. Five years ago, she discovered Naughty-n-Nice, where she met Davis and eventually became his accountant. Since then, she had been helping Davis make his illegal business look legal on the money side of things. She began helping elsewhere, recently even talking to the young but still of-age girls Davis was interested in under the alias Erika Sin. When Melanie had the idea to start camming, she helped her and even encouraged her to go and work for Davis. Planning on eventually taking large cuts of the money her daughter made to fill in some of the voids their lifestyle had created.

Then, she threw a cheap excuse at me, "Men want a young, naïve, innocent, skinny, fertile playful thing. They don't want an old, experienced, fat woman like me with all my stretch marks and wrinkles."

"I did," I snarled at her.

She took my response and used it as an opportunity to plead with me one last time. "You do still love me, don't you, Josh? We can get out of here. You can pick me up and carry me out of here. You can do whatever you want to me. We never have to come back here again. We can go somewhere else and build a life together. What are you waiting for, Josh? Let's go."

I stood there towering above her. This was it. It was the last time I was going to see her, and it was the last time she was going to see me. My last words to her simply were, "Lady, go die."

Andy Lind

Andy Lind is a third shift factory worker by night, but by day, he is a writer of romance, suspense, mystery, and a combination of all three. He lives in Rockford, Illinois, but spends most of his free time traveling up and down The Mississippi River.

A SPECIAL THANK YOU TO YOU!

On behalf of everyone at Freedom Of Speech Publishing, thank you for choosing Whom Gods Destroy for your reading enjoyment.

As an added bonus and special thank you, for purchasing Whom Gods Destroy, you can enjoy discounts and special promotions on other Freedom of Speech Publishing products. Visit freedomofspeechpublishing.com/vip to learn more.

We are committed to providing you with the highest level of customer satisfaction possible. If for any reason you have questions or comments, we are delighted to hear from you. Email us at cs@freedomofspeechpublishing.com or visit our website at: http://freedomofspeechpublishing.com/contact-us-2/.

If you enjoyed Whom Gods Destroy, visit www.freedomofspeechpublishing.com for a list of similar books or upcoming books.

Again, thank you for your patronage. We look forward to providing you more entertainment in the future.

WHOM GODS DESTROY
By Andy Lind

www.ingramcontent.com/pod-product-compliance
Lightning Source LLC
Chambersburg PA
CBHW051545030726
47592CB00001B/146